revealers

ALSO BY
AMANDA MARRONE

Uninvited

revealers

AMANDA MARRONE

SIMON PULSE · New York · London · Toronto · Sydney

SIMON PULSE

An imprint of Simon & Schuster Children's Publishing Division

1230 Avenue of the Americas, New York, NY 10020

Copyright © 2008 by Amanda Marrone

All rights reserved, including the right of

reproduction in whole or in part in any form.

SIMON PULSE and colophon are registered

trademarks of Simon & Schuster, Inc.

Designed by Jessica Sonkin

The text of this book was set in Adobe Garamond.

Manufactured in the United States of America

First Simon Pulse edition September 2008

2 4 6 8 10 9 7 5 3

Library of Congress Control Number 2007943083

ISBN-13: 978-1-4169-5874-1

ISBN-10: 1-4169-5874-6

To Nina Nelson, Pam Foarde,
and Kelsey Johnson Defatte
for support above and beyond the call of duty!
I couldn't have done this without you—

Thanks to my fabulous editor, Jen Klonsky, for helping me hash out the details; my wonderful agent, Wendy Schmalz, for taking me on; and my critique group, Nina, Pam, Naomi, and Rob—and online—Kelsey, for helping me write this. My husband, Joe, who made this all possible, and Max and Merry who tried to be patient while I was writing this. Thanks to all the folks at Simon Pulse, and Griffin, my very first dog, who provided unconditional love when I needed it.

revealers

1

I wake and turn to my window. The witch ball is rattling against the inside of the pane, glowing from a tangled spell within. I wonder which one of my so-called friends threw a hex my way? I watch the spell dance around in the spun glass, and hear the swoosh of brooms flying past, capes flapping. One, two, three soft landings rustle the leaves by the back door. The fourth hits the dirt hard, and I smile, thinking Dani better stop scarfing doughnuts or she won't be able to get off the ground much longer.

The ball bursts apart and glass clatters against the baseboard. Margo. Damn her, she's always breaking them. I'll have to ask Mom to make the next one stronger.

I get out of bed and throw on a sweatshirt and jeans. I hope I'll be able to find a hat because it's getting too damn cold flying around on the stupid sticks without one. The last time I suggested we take a car, Zahara practically bit my head off—"We go by air or we don't go at all!" Like she's such the traditionalist. Ha! Wonder what her mother will say when she notices the tongue stud she's sporting?

By the time I get downstairs, they're already walking into the kitchen. I wish my mom would keep the door locked or put up a do-not-enter spell, if only to keep Margo stewing out in the cold for a few minutes.

Dani waves at me. "Hey, Jules."

Sascha kneels and Nuisance jumps up in her arms, nuzzling his chin against her, purring madly.

I scan their faces—only Margo and Zahara seemed pissed. Their cheeks are bright red, and I breathe the smoky night air they brought in with them. "Hey, guys."

Zahara clacks her tongue stud on her front teeth, and runs her hand across her close-cropped black hair. "Nice bed head. Apparently you didn't know we were coming."

I run my fingers through my curls and look at the cauldron bubbling furiously on the burner—deep-purple steam flying up to the vent. "Mom! Why didn't you wake me up?"

My mom pads into the room and casts a glance at the pot. "Again? Didn't you girls go out a few nights ago?"

Margo rolls her eyes and snorts. "Um, it's not like they run on a schedule or anything."

Mom gives a half smile and shrugs. I hate she's taking that from Margo, but I'm no better. The more Margo and Zahara vie for Queen Bee, the more the rest of us seem to shrink in their wake. Well, not Sascha. Sascha seems to float outside the circle, only stepping in when things are about to break. But when did this happen to us? When did the need to pull rank get so strong?

Mom sighs as she heads to the stove. "There've been a lot more than usual." She reaches into a jar and tosses some herbs into the water until the steam runs clear. "Do you know who it is?" she asks.

Sascha nods. "Yeah, it's the guy who gutted that Wilkins lady last week. They tracked him down. Should be an easy job. Mrs. Keyes said he's at that bar by the river so we should get going before he drinks too much and passes out."

My mom cocks her head and purses her lips. "Sorry I wasn't keeping an eye on it, girls. There's a really good movie on and well, I guess I was hoping you'd get a few nights off."

Dani flicks her eyes at Margo and Zahara—then flashes a tiny smile at my mom. "It's okay, Mrs. Harris, my mom didn't see it right away, either."

"But she did see it," Margo says. "We didn't have to come fetch you."

"We're all together now," Sascha says quietly. "Let's just go."

"I need to find a hat first." I grab my wool cape from the coat rack and open the closet.

"For God's sake," Zahara says, "it's not that cold!"

I give her a hard look but close the door. "Fine."

Sascha squeezes my hand with icy fingers as we head to the mudroom. "You're going to wish you had a hat—it is *that* cold."

Of course Sascha wouldn't be caught dead in a hat—she totally gets off on her long black hair swirling behind her as we ride. Like anyone is watching. But me, I'll take warmth over vanity, and it's not like a hat could make a dent in my curls.

"Bye, girls," my mom calls. "Be careful."

I fasten my cape, grab my broom, and follow them out. Sascha was right—it's freaking cold. The wind whips around my face sucking the warm air away. "Just a minute." As I head back into the house my broom jerks in my hand ready to fly, and I clutch the smooth handle to keep from losing my grip. I rummage through the bins in the closet and snag my purple hat.

When I get back outside, Zahara's jaw is clenched tight—I hear her clacking the tongue stud impatiently on her teeth.

Margo smirks. "That's *real* stylish!"

I pull the wool down over my ears. "Thanks!"

We mount our sticks, and Sascha says, "I'll do it." She

shakes her long hair so it fans out around her shoulders. *"We fly in darkness for the good of all, let us pass unseen till we land again."*

A shimmering fog envelops us and we're off. I tip my broom toward the sky and rise up. The frigid air cuts through my cape and I make a mental note to get my heavy sweaters down from the attic.

Margo flies alongside me. "Your mother needs to get it together. Helena isn't going to tolerate this crap."

"Yeah, well, I wonder what *Helena* would think if she knew you were throwing her first name around like you're best buds? I was under the impression we were to call her 'Mrs. Keyes.' You broke another ball, by the way! What the hell were you trying to do?"

Margo looks down her thin pointy nose with wide eyes. "It was just a joke—the worst it could've done was give you a good jolt. And as of this weekend I'll be part of the inner circle, and I'm sure Mrs. Keyes will *insist* I use her first name." She grins, points her broom down, and shoots ahead next to Zahara.

I look behind, and pull my broom to fall back next to Dani. "Hey," I say. "How's it going?"

Dani shakes her head. "I've got a stupid chem test first period tomorrow. I really should be studying right now."

"Sorry I was late. I pulled an all-nighter yesterday and I crashed early tonight."

"It's okay, but Margo got all bent we had to come get you. Of course her mom is always watching their cauldron—always kissing ass."

I laugh, glad to have Dani by my side—on my side.

We ride a ways in silence and then I turn to her. "Things are so weird lately. I'm always afraid I'll say something wrong and piss Margo or Z off."

Dani nods. "We're supposed to be in this together, but . . ." She shrugs and looks ahead at Margo and Zahara. "My mom said this happened to them, too. She said it always does—I mean, there's only so long a bunch of girls can hang without getting on each other's nerves. But we have to try to keep it together. There's no one to take our places yet."

"They're making it harder to want to stay together."

Dani points her chin skyward. "Look at Miss Priss."

Sascha's flying higher than the rest of us—back stick-straight—hair stretching out behind her. "One good gust and she's gonna get blown off riding like that."

Dani draws in closer to me. "Connor's on cleanup tonight."

"I figured," I say, hoping I sound like I don't care.

Dani knows how much I like Connor, though. Of course, seeing as Connor and Michael are the only guys our age in the coven, there isn't a whole lot of choice. But Connor and I were inseparable until we hit seventh grade, and then our moms made it clear we needed some distance. I started hanging out with Dani, and Connor spent more time with Michael, but whenever we're together he sticks by my side and I hope he still thinks about me as much as I think about him.

"Who's helping?" I ask, hoping it's not Zahara's dad. All he does is complain about how bad his back is and how he really shouldn't be out at night in the cold.

Dani sticks out her tongue. "Michael. Let's hope he put some deodorant on today."

"Come on—Michael's a sweetie!"

"I know he is, but why haven't his parents told him his pits stink? I'd do it, but I don't want to hurt his feelings."

Sascha cuts down in front of us and points toward the parking lot. "There they are."

I nod as we circle the lot and land next to Connor's van. The glamour hiding us blows away as soon as our feet touch the ground. Connor puts the window down. "Hey, what took you so long?"

Margo rolls her eyes. "What do you think? I hope your mom won't be upset."

Connor winks at me, and my stomach flips. "Don't worry, Jules, all she cares about is getting the job done. I'll call Michael; he's been buying the guy drinks inside."

I glance at Margo, her frown illuminated by the bar's neon sign, and try not to smile.

Connor punches the button on his cell phone and waits. "Hey! They're here."

"Why don't we head toward the river?" I say. As much as I'd love to stay with Connor, I need to concentrate on what we're doing.

Zahara nods and turns toward the sound of the water. "I'll bind him," she says to Margo.

Margo reaches into her cape and pulls out a small bag. "Here ya go." She turns to me as we wind our way through the trees. "Did you finish your *Beowulf* questions?"

"Yeah."

"Can I copy them before class? I was too busy making binders for *Mrs. Keyes*."

"I guess."

Dani tugs on my sleeve, and rolls her eyes. I'm pretty sure we're thinking the same thing—Margo's a kiss ass like her mother.

"Thanks," Margo says. "It took forever just to get a dozen done. I forgot how hard it is to roll the stupid things into a ball, and the damn paper is so thin it kept ripping when I tried twisting the top closed."

"It's got to be thin," Dani says, "so it'll break open when you throw it."

Margo glares at Dani and I know she's gonna give her shit for her habit of overstating the obvious. "Like I don't know

8

that! I was just saying they're a pain in the ass to make!"

Dani purses her lips for a second, looking embarrassed. "Sorry."

Sascha puts her hand on Margo's shoulder. "This is a good spot."

We form a semicircle and wait. The river is full and noisy tonight—I hope it'll be enough to mask the sound.

"Here they come," Dani whispers.

"I want you to know I've never done this before," a man's voice says in the dark.

"Me neither," Michael says.

They come around a tree and he sees us.

"What the fu—"

"We bind you to the earth!" Zahara yells as she throws the wound paper to the ground at the man's feet. The ball bursts in a shower of blue light. Dirt, sticks, and decaying leaves bind together into snakelike tendrils, wrapping around his feet and twisting up his legs and around his waist to hold him in place.

I see him cover his round face as I blink away the echoes of light from my eyes. We draw closer to him—our arms stretched out to the sides to form a circle, energy leaping from our fingertips keeping the circle strong in case he's able to break free.

"What the hell's going on?" he asks, squinting at us. "Mike?"

"I'll go get the bag," Michael says, heading to the van.

"Hey, Mike!" The man struggles to move his feet. "Where are you going? Don't leave me."

"We hear you're a very naughty boy when the full moon comes out." Margo laughs.

"Let's just get on with it," Sascha says, sounding bored.

"Look, I don't know what you're talking about. I was just coming out here for—"

He pauses and I wonder what Michael said to get him to come with him. Puffs of breath leave his mouth in short bursts. He pulls at his knees but the forest floor holds him tight.

"We have reason to believe you're responsible for some recent werewolf activity," Zahara says like she's a cop. "What do you have to say for yourself?"

"Shit," he says. "Look, I've never hurt anyone. I take precautions."

Zahara scoffs. "Funny, I think Annie Wilkins and Steven Gardener would beg to differ—if they were still alive, that is."

"Steven was before I got a watcher. And, and—Annie, that was an accident, I swear. I—I liked Annie—I never would've hurt her on purpose. Something went wrong, but it'll never happen again."

Margo nods her head. "Damn straight it'll never happen again."

"Come on," Sascha says, "let's just get this over with."

"He needs to show some remorse!" Zahara snaps.

Margo looks at Z. "When do they ever show remorse?"

"Oh, my God, you're part of that group, aren't you? Oh, God no. I'll leave town, please," he begs. "Just let me go!"

Tears glisten on his cheeks. I hate when we drag it out like this, I hate how I start feeling sorry for them.

Zahara sighs. "All right, fine, let's do it."

The man smiles—he must think Z was talking about letting him go.

We all face our palms toward him and yell, "*Reveal!*"

Yellow light swirls around him forming a ball above his head. He looks at the sky with wide terrified eyes. I know he's feeling the change coming and instinctively searching for the round moon that isn't there.

"What did you do to me? This shouldn't be happening—it's not time!" he screams. "Please, just give me another chance!"

I want to look away but I never do. I need to see the change so I can steel myself for what comes next.

His face twists and expands into a long snout. I'm glad the water crashing behind us drowns the groan of bones growing at a remarkable pace. His clothes tear and drop. I get a glimpse between his legs, and feel my cheeks flush. Dark coarse hair grows, covering him, and he's complete. He snarls at us, jerking his muzzle from one person to the next, swiping the air with razor claws.

I reach into my cape pocket and take out my gun, freshly loaded with silver bullets. Arm straight—I aim at his chest and fire. We all step back to avoid the spray as he goes down. I don't watch his body change back, I want to remember him as the wolf and not the man—it makes it easier to sleep at night.

Michael walks past with the body bag. "Nice work."

"Anyone want to hang for a bit?" Connor asks as he helps Michael spread the bag.

Margo smiles. "Love to!"

Zahara lifts a flask from her cape. She takes a swig and hands it to Margo. "Me, too. We could head back to your house, Connor. Margo's got a bunch of binders to give your mom."

Connor looks at me. "How about you, Jules?"

I shrug, feeling drained. "I should head home; I'm tired and it's late."

He pouts his lips, and I almost change my mind, but Zahara and Margo exchange looks, and I don't feel like dealing with any more of their crap tonight.

"Hey, Michael, what did you tell the guy to get him out here?" I ask, changing the subject.

Michael looks up and winks at me. "Blow job."

Shaking my head, I take the flask from Margo. The cool metal stings my lips as the brandy burns its way down my throat. I hate the way it tastes, but Zahara refuses to fill the flask with wine or anything else because "brandy is the traditional after-kill drink." Of course it doesn't help having Helena in charge, making sure things are ridiculously old school.

I hand it to Dani who takes a quick sip. "I've got a chem quiz."

Sascha holds out her hand and takes the flask. "I've got a French translation to finish." She takes a long drink and puts the flask in her cape. "You don't mind if I borrow this do you, Z? My mom noticed some of her booze was missing, and she cast a spell on all the bottles so they'll only open for her. But I'm going to need a little buzz to help me get through interpreting *Le Petite Prince, c'est tres difficile pour moi*!"

"Okay," Zahara say, "but don't drink the whole thing—I don't want Mrs. Keyes on my ass for going through her good brandy too quickly!"

She shoots an apologetic look at Connor, but he just smiles. He knows what a bitch his mom can be.

Sascha pats the flask in her cape. "Don't worry, a little goes a long way." She mounts her broom and heads up through the trees. "Later."

Michael and Connor grunt as they roll the man into the bag.

"What was his name?" I ask.

Michael wipes his sleeve across his forehead. "Uh, Jack."

Connor zips the bag up and stands, wiping his hands against his jeans.

I look up at the sharp crescent moon. "Rest in peace, Jack."

Connor laughs. "You're such a softy, Jules! You sure you can't hang with us?"

"If she's tired, she's tired," Margo says.

Dani sighs. I wonder if she's waiting for Connor to ask her to come over, too. She crosses her arms across her stomach. "Well, like I said, I've got to study." She leans in and kisses everyone on the cheek, something we used to do all the time—now it looks awkward and forced.

"I'll go with you," I say, air-kissing Margo and Zahara. I squeeze Michael's shoulder, and then I put one hand on Connor's cheek and give him a long, wet, full-on-the-mouth kiss. He presses my lips with his and I pull away.

"Bye," I whisper. I mount my broom—my heart pounding louder than the water on the rocks. I look at Zahara and Margo, and try very hard not to smile in their wide-eyed faces. "Have fun, guys."

As we clear the parking lot, Dani bursts out laughing. "Oh, my God, Jules—you so rule! I can't believe you did that. Did you see their faces? Did you? And he totally kissed you back!"

I allow the smile to come now and wonder if he can taste brandy on his lips. I just hope there won't be hell to pay tomorrow.

2

I walk into the kitchen, and I'm relieved to see the cauldron steam is still clear—it's rare we get called out twice in a night, but the way things are going lately, I wouldn't be surprised.

The kitchen air warms my hands, stiff from clutching the broom. I check my cape for blood, and then drape it on a chair.

"I'm home."

Mom shuffles in, wrapped in a thick blue bathrobe with Nuisance winding between her legs. "Sorry about earlier, I should've been paying closer attention."

"They could call, too. It's totally archaic watching for the steam to turn color 24/7."

"You know Helena likes to keep as many of the old ways in place as possible."

"Well, it's idiotic." I pull out the chair from the table, and pat my lap until Nuisance jumps up.

"Did things go smoothly?"

"Yeah, but he knew about us." I try to erase his voice pleading with us from my head.

"Word gets around. These *things* network, and warn each other."

"So you'd think he would've left town long ago."

Mom shakes her head. "No one ever claimed wolves were smart."

Nuisance sniffs my cape, and jumps to the floor. "No one ever said they smell good, either." I walk to the coat rack and hang my cape up, and then open the closet to get the dustpan and a broom. "Margo cast some spell on her way over and broke the ball. Can you make me another? A stronger one?"

"You could take a crack at making one yourself. It's been ages since you tried."

"Uh, it's been ages because I loathe glassblowing—it's too hot and I can't get the glass to form a ball, let alone work any threads inside."

Mom laughs. "They *were* pretty bad. I was planning on being in the studio tomorrow, anyway. I'm experimenting with a new type of ball for Helena. I'll blow a couple with thicker walls and extra threads for you."

"Experimenting?"

"We have some ideas about other ways we might be able to use the balls. If I can get them to work, they might send the coven in a new direction."

"If it puts us in the twenty-first century, then I'm on board."

"Not everyone minds following the old ways."

"Yeah, but not everyone's a kiss ass like Zahara and Margo."

"Watch the language!"

"Sorry, but sometimes I just don't see the point. The world around us keeps moving on, and we're stuck hunting night-mares the same way it was done three hundred years ago."

"It's because of us the world *can* move on."

"Yeah, yeah—without us the world would be plagued by creatures—blah, blah, blah. The way I see it, we're only making a small dent in the monster population in our little corner of Connecticut."

Mom looks at me like I'm three, and she's about to explain the ins and outs of the coven for the first time.

"I know—anything we kill makes a difference and saves lives," I say.

"Right, and an old-fashioned stake in the heart gets the job done, so what's to change?"

I put the dustpan down on the table and sit opposite Mom. "Nothing, I guess, but when you were hunting, did you ever want to quit and just lead a normal life?"

"This is normal—for us. But yes, sometimes it got hard seeing the other girls at school, knowing they were sleeping soundly at night, going out with boys, never worrying about the right way to stake a vampire. Of course none of that was as hard as sending you out for your first hunt."

"Gee, what was so hard about sending your kid out to kill a vampire? It's not like you could've known the thing would mesmerize Dani and Sascha into uselessness, and we'd break four stakes before Zahara managed to drive one home, right? But then again, we were only *thirteen*!"

"You had practice."

"Spiking a hay bale is not the same thing as dusting a vamp with superhuman strength."

Mom rubs her eyes and yawns. "It gives you the right resistance, though—so you'd know how much force you'd need to get the stake in."

"I guess I should be thankful it wasn't a werewolf, or I'd have been hunted down before I morphed into a wolf during the next full moon!"

"Oh, stop being such a drama queen. You never make wolves reveal themselves unless they're bound to the spot and out of biting range! But I'll let you in on a little secret."

"What?" I ask, sounding bored.

Mom reaches across the table and puts her hand over mine. "The first couple of months—we were watching you, and ready to step in if things got out of control."

I pull my hand away and give her an incredulous look. "You didn't think things got a little out of control on our first hunt? I ended up with fifteen stitches before we managed to stake Miss Melissa!"

I shake my head. I can still vividly remember the shooting pain I got when our story-time librarian, Miss Melissa, dragged her new teeth across my shoulder after my stake splintered against her sternum. I remember the crazed look in her eyes as she lashed out at us with clawed fingers. And Dani literally peed in her pants, something Margo still gives her crap about.

"If you had known we were there," Mom continues, "you might've held back, thinking we'd step in. As I recall, you were all pretty darned happy when you got to Helena's house."

"We were pretty darned happy because we were still alive!" Well, we were happy until Helena had us each take a swig of brandy. Sascha was the only one who didn't gag, but if I bring up how wrong it was giving booze to eighth graders, we'll just get into the whole "it's just a tradition" talk again.

At any rate, I'm just not sure this is what I want to do with my life."

"You only have to do it until the next generation is ready to take over."

"Yeah, that's another thing—what if I don't want to get

19

married and have a kid who'll have to take over hunting? Maybe I like girls, or maybe I want to do more with my life—like be a vet or something. Seriously, helping sick puppies sounds way better than plugging werewolves at close range."

Mom purses her lips, and I know I've headed into "you'll understand everything when you turn eighteen" territory. "Sweetie, you just need to hang on a little longer. Your birthday is only two months away—you'll be a part of the inner circle, and your future and your place in the coven will be clear. You'll understand."

She gets up and turns off the light over the stove top. "Look, it's late—why don't you head up to bed?"

I start up the stairs, and then lean over the rail. "I kissed Connor tonight. And he kissed me back!" Mom's eyes widen, and I see panic on her face for a split second before she narrows her eyes. Why can't I keep my mouth shut?

She takes a deep breath like she's trying to keep her cool. "Julia, just keep your nose in your books and on our mission, and stay away from Connor. When the time is right you'll find someone to be with. Maybe it will be Connor, but now is not the time."

"In case you hadn't noticed, I have a mind of my own, and who's to say the time isn't now?" I stomp up the stairs, figuring if she's going to treat me like a three-year-old, I might as well act like one.

I slam my door, throw the dustpan and broom on the floor, and flop on my bed. I'm so sick of the secrets—of everything. Why can't they tell us what's going on? We're seventeen years old—what's so magical about eighteen?

And where does the coven get off saying when I can be with someone? The whole idea of us having the next generation of hunters at the same time is insane!

I'm tempted to ignore the broken glass, but then I think Nuisance might get into it. I get up and start sweeping the debris into the dustpan, and jump when something hits my window. I turn off the light and look out. Connor is standing outside, motioning to me.

I put my hand on the window, my heart pounding as my mom's words echo in my head. I wave at him—not sure he can see me, and then run my fingers through my hair. I walk back to my door and twist the knob with a shaking hand.

I listen at the top of the stairs, and hear muffled voices coming from the TV.

I lick my lips and whisper, "I fly in darkness for the good of all, let me pass unseen till I land again." My shadow disappears from the wall as the fog envelopes me. I steal down the steps, grimacing every time the wood squeaks. Nuisance looks up from his cat bed when I reach the bottom, and I wonder if I'm invisible to animals, too.

I slip out the back door and walk to the side of the house. Connor is looking up at my window. "Jules? Are you there? Jules?" he calls out softly.

I tiptoe my way over to him, cover his eyes with my hands, and whisper, "Boo!"

He turns around and laughs, reaching out for me, and I step to the side as his fingers graze my arm. He lunges in my direction and slaps his hand across my butt.

"Hey, watch it!"

"If I can't see you, it's not my fault if I grab something I'm not supposed to!" He reaches out and swipes the air inches in front of me. "But there's something cool about kissing an invisible girl!"

I step back and a stick snaps under my foot. Connor jumps forward and wraps his arms around my waist. He leans in and his lips brush against my cheek.

I reveal myself, and halfheartedly push him away. "Who said anything about kissing? And what are you doing here anyway?"

Connor lets me go and steps back. The cold air rushes between us, and I wish I were still in his arms. "My mom kicked Margo and Z out because it's a school night—that and she's researching some spell." He gives me a crooked smile and my legs feel wobbly. "As for the kissing part—you started it. I just came by to see if you wanted to continue."

This time I let him take me in his arms. I tilt my chin up and his cool lips press into mine. How many times have I dreamed about this? How many times have I been told it could never happen?

"We shouldn't be doing this," I whisper.

"That's part of the fun."

"What if my mom catches us—or your mother finds out?"

He leans in and kisses me again, his mouth lingering on my lower lip. "Since when do you care about the rules?"

I pull away from him and take a step back. "Is that why you're here? Because you think out of all of us, I'd be the one who wouldn't care about breaking the rules?"

He reaches out and takes my hand. "Jules, you know it's always been you I liked—and after that kiss tonight I was pretty sure we were on the same page."

I want to believe him; I want it to be true. "But your mom—"

"My mom needs a wake-up call—you and I know things can't stay the same forever."

A strong gust blows past us. "Come on." I lead Connor to my mom's studio in the backyard. I reach up for the key resting on the sill and open the door. The air inside is cold and smells like stale smoke. I take him to the couch facing the window overlooking the pond. Dozens of glass balls hanging from the curtain rod glitter in the moonlight, and I hold my hand up to one. "*Light*," I whisper. My spell catches in the glass threads inside the ball, bathing us in a soft blue glow.

"Are you sure about this?" I ask.

Connor reaches out, pulls me down, and takes me in his arms. "I'll fight for you if I have to." He buries his face into my neck and I breathe in his sandalwood cologne. Our legs wrap around each other's, and every inch of my skin feels alive for the first time. Why have we let them keep us apart?

He kisses my ear—his teeth lingering on my earlobe. I press my hips into his and think the coven is long overdue for a change.

3

I'm walking past the peach-colored lockers with a shit-eating grin on my face. I usually cast a cloaking spell to keep me out of focus in the halls, but today I want everyone to see me—to see I'm different. Kids who usually ignore me, even when I'm out in the open, are shooting looks my way. I stare them in the eye and suppress the urge to say *I was with Connor Keyes last night!* A shiver runs up my spine just thinking about it—about him—and what we did.

Part of me is a little worried about facing Margo and Zahara—like they might figure it out just by looking at me. When I push through the doors to the quad and see them at our table in the far corner, I make a mental note to forget the feel of Connor's bare skin on mine—to play it cool.

Margo spots me and waves. "Jules! Where have you been? Class is gonna start in fifteen minutes."

I sit across from her, and hand over my *Beowulf* questions. "I'm guessing you were looking for these?"

"Yeah!" Margo says, snatching my homework. She stares into my face and smiles. "You look like crap."

"I love how you butter me up when you need to copy my work. I didn't get much sleep last night, okay?" *Because I was up hooking up with Connor.*

"Tell me about it," Zahara says. "I never sleep well after killing wolves—I just lie in bed and keep picturing their faces changing—ugh."

"So, did you guys have fun at Connor's?" I ask, trying not to smirk.

Margo looks up from her paper. "Totally!"

Zahara rolls her eyes. "Mrs. Keyes kicked us out after five minutes. She's working on some spell to use with your mom's witch balls."

"What I meant," Margo says, "is we had a blast before we went *over* to his house. Connor was packing up the van and was telling us about this witch who visited his mom because she was interested in joining the coven—you know—total Wiccan-love-spell-magik with a *k* loser. Apparently she almost fainted when Mrs. Keyes told her what we do! And—if you can believe it, Michael wasn't in total dork mode. He was actually kind of funny."

26

"She's right," Z adds. "And I think someone gave Michael the heads-up about the body odor problem. I could stand next to him without having to breathe through my mouth."

I notice Margo staring at something behind me, and turn. Dani's walking with Evan Klein. I look back at Margo, and watch her upper lip draw into a sneer.

"You need to talk to Dani," she says.

"She was probably studying for her chem test with him. Nothing to get all twisted about."

Zahara takes a quick peek. "No, she's right. Dani's been hanging with him a lot, and we all know she's got zero will-power. She's so needy and starved for affection—can you imagine her saying *no* if he asks her out?"

"The point could be made," I say, "that we're all starved for attention."

Margo narrows her eyes. "But Dani's weak." She points a finger at Evan and blows on it. "Gee, I feel a chill in the air. I hope Evan doesn't slip on a patch of ice."

Evan trips and goes sprawling to the ground. The quad fills with snickers as a flutter of papers rains down on him.

"Oops!" Margo says.

"Was that necessary?" I ask.

Margo sighs. "Maybe not, but it was fun and it got her attention."

Dani's staring at us as she helps Evan up. I brace myself

in case she decides to throw a spell back our way, but she just scowls and starts picking up papers.

"What got whose attention?" Sascha asks, placing a tray on the table next to Margo. She flips her hair back and hands out coffees. I hold the cup in both hands to warm my fingers.

"Dani's," Margo says. "She's been spending a lot time with that dorky Evan, and I kind of tripped him up."

Sascha shakes her head, fanning her hair around her shoulders. "Save the spells for obnoxious cheerleaders. Dani knows guys are off-limits, and seeing as Mrs. Keyes scares the shit out of her, I don't think she's going to do anything that would get her sent in for a *talk*."

"Unlike some people." Zahara turns to me.

"What?" I will my cheeks not to turn red, and meet Z's dark brown eyes with what I hope is a combined look of innocence and ignorance.

"You and Connor were a little friendly last night."

"Did I miss something good?" Sascha asks, leaning in.

My cheeks flush, and I study the top of my coffee cup—if they only knew the half of it. "No."

Zahara throws her head back and laughs. "Yes! Jules gave Connor one freaking monster of a good-night kiss—she practically stuck her tongue down his throat."

"I did not stick my tongue down his throat!" *That you know about.*

28

"I, for one, was embarrassed for you," Margo says. "Unless you want the guys in the coven thinking you're a tease?"

"All two of them?" Sascha asks.

"Margo, honey, you're just mad you didn't try it first," Zahara says.

Margo's eyes go wide and I'm tempted to high-five Zahara. I hate to admit it, but part of me totally gets off when those two go at it—especially if it takes the attention off me.

"Unlike *some* people," Margo says, "I don't have any desire to break the rules."

"You mean the rules designed to suck the fun out of our lives?" Sascha asks. She sits up straight and narrows her eyes. "A good hunter keeps her distance from non-coven people," she says with a touch of ice in her voice—doing a dead-on imitation of Mrs. Keyes.

"A good hunter keeps herself chaste," Z adds.

"A good hunter will explode from lack of contact with the opposite sex," Sascha deadpans.

Margo shakes her head in disgust. "A good hunter will cut the crap and do what she's supposed to do."

"God, Margo," Zahara says. "Lighten up."

"You should talk!" she says. "The way you were grilling that wolf last night was a little much."

"Keep it down," Sascha says. "Besides, there are ways to get around the rules."

"Like what?" I ask, hoping whatever she says can help Connor and me.

"Well, we're not supposed to mess around with coven guys, right? You know, until it's time for the unnatural group birthing the coven has planned—but they never said we couldn't fool around with guys from *other* covens. Remember the solstice gathering last June?"

Zahara smiles knowingly.

Margo looks back and forth between them. "Oh, my God! Did you two hook up?"

Sascha's lips curl up ever so slightly. "Let's just say that hotty from the Massachusetts coven—Kyle, the one in the Hawaiian shirt—knows his way around in the dark."

"Guy with the black dreads," Zahara says. "Smokin' kisser, but I'll be damned if I can remember his name."

They turn to me and I shrug. "Uh, I hung out with Dani and Michael that night—and seeing as it was, like, eighty degrees out, Michael's stench kept most everyone away."

"OK, which one of you tripped Evan?"

Dani's standing at the end of the table—she asked all of us the question, but her eyes are locked on Margo's.

"It was just a joke," Margo says.

I move over so Dani can sit down. Sascha hands her a coffee.

"Well, it wasn't funny. I have to pass this test and he was

helping me until he fell. He had to go to the nurse for a bandage and an ice pack."

"Baby," Margo whispers.

"He ripped a hole in his pants and got blood all over the place!"

Margo shakes her head. "Sorry, I didn't know you two were that close."

"We're not! It was—uh, just for the test, you know?" Dani sputters. "And—and did you ever think we call more attention to ourselves by *keeping to ourselves*, instead of actually, like, talking to other people?"

Zahara opens her mouth to speak, but Sascha taps a finger to her lip—her signal that she thinks she has something important to say. "You know," she says, moving her finger to point at the rest of the quad, "Dani isn't totally off base with this one."

Dani sits up straight, giving Margo an I-told-you-so smile.

"If you think about it," she continues, "the more we stay apart, the more we might elicit curiosity among some of our more inquisitive classmates."

"Like Evan's friend, Finn," Zahara says. "He's always checking us out. I keep wondering if he somehow knows what we are."

I nod, thinking about all the times I've cloaked myself in the halls—usually everyone flows around me—like they're aware of something moving in the halls, but they don't really see it. But a couple of times Finn has walked right up to me, and I had to swerve at the last second to avoid a collision. And I've caught him staring at Sascha before. She's beautiful, so normally that wouldn't be so strange, except most of the kids here *do* ignore us.

"And then on the opposite side of the spectrum," Sascha says, "we've got Brooke Brennan, who wouldn't notice us if we flew into homeroom on our brooms." She takes a sip of coffee and then gives Margo a knowing look. "Let's get back to boys! Margo, can you really tell us you've never let a guy cop a feel?"

Margo's mouth drops open for a second, then she wrinkles her pointy nose. "No!"

Dani turns to me—eyebrows raised. "We've been discussing the *no boys* rule," I say, "and how you can get around it."

Dani blushes. "Uh."

"Articulate as ever," Margo says. "But I'm sure we can put you in the play-by-the-rules category."

Dani looks like she's not sure if that's a good thing or a bad thing.

"And to make sure you stay there," Margo adds, "I suggest you avoid Evan. The guy looks as desperate as you do—I can just picture the sparks flying over the periodic table."

Margo hands my homework back and tilts her head toward Zahara. "Let's get to class, Z."

"I'm coming, too," Sascha says. "I want to hear more about Dreadlock Boy."

Dani and I sip our coffee and watch them walk into the building.

"I hate her," Dani says when the door shuts behind them. "And we were just studying."

"I know," I say, even though it's painfully obvious Dani does have it bad for Evan. I get up, sling my backpack over my shoulder, and head for the door. "Connor came over last night." My heart flutters as I let the big smile return to my face.

Dani rushes up next to me. "What? Why? Well, I can guess why—but what happened?"

"He wanted to see me, and we kind of—you know."

"Oh, my God, Jules, you didn't?"

I shake my head. "We didn't do *it*, if that's what you're thinking—but we—well, you know. Stuff happened."

Dani's smiling back at me, and I'm so relieved she didn't get all Margo-coven-cop on me. "*Stuff*?"

"Yeah, you know—'I don't know if I'll be able to look him in the eye today' kind of stuff. Seriously, I don't know if I can. My stomach is in knots waiting to see him. We can't go public yet—you know with all the stupid rules—but the important part is he wants to."

Dani tugs on my sleeve and points at the bathroom.

We open the door and she bends down to look under the stalls. "Just one," she whispers. *Cloak?* she mouths.

I nod and whisper the cloaking spell just in case it's someone really obnoxious we don't feel like dealing with.

The toilet flushes and we watch some freshman pick food out of her teeth instead of washing her hands. Dani wrinkles her nose, and sticks out her tongue.

When the girl leaves, I twirl my finger in a spiral. "Why can't the teachers monitor the damn bathrooms—I can't stand breathing this in! *Vanish*," I say, pointing toward a sink. The cigarette smoke hanging in the air pulls together into a funnel cloud and disappears down the drain. I smile in the mirror and check my teeth.

"I'm in love with Evan," Dani blurts out.

"What?" I ask, trying to sound surprised.

"I know, I know—keep away from boys, especially non-coven boys—but I like him so much, and every time I'm with him I practically pass out. And yesterday he asked me for my cell number—and I gave it to him."

"Hey, Helena can't come down on you for just giving a guy your number—especially if you're just getting together to *study*."

Dani giggles and blushes. "Oh, he can study me anytime he wants." She looks in the mirror and then reaches into her purse for some face powder. "Actually," she says, dusting her nose, "between the hunt and me staring at my phone hoping he'd call last night, I should probably cut my first class and do some real studying."

"And they say romance is dead."

"Seriously, my mom will kill me if I bomb this test." She lifts her bangs and swipes the brush across her forehead, and then breaks out in a huge smile. "Oh, God, who am I kidding? I don't even care anymore. All I can think about is what am I gonna to do if he calls?"

"Not if—when!"

Dani gives me a sly look. "We should run away—leave the stupid coven and the stupid rules behind. We can hang out with our taboo boyfriends by day and be hunters by night."

"Who says we'd keeping hunting?" I ask.

"Could you live with yourself knowing there were vamps and such running around?"

I shake my head. "I guess not, but have you thought about what Evan would think if he knew your after-school job involves killing monsters instead of flipping burgers?"

Dani slings her backpack over one shoulder and looks me in the eye. "As a matter of fact, I have. In my fantasy world, Evan is very supportive and always has doughnuts waiting for an after-kill treat. He lovingly sharpens my stakes, and rolls binders for me. I also imagine him coming up with some cool techno ways to track the bad guys—when we're not practicing martial arts together, that is."

We both laugh. "In mine, Connor just tells his mother to shove it and we move to Canada, where there aren't so many nightmares."

"Actually, there's that nasty black arts coven in Montreal—not to mention more than a few werewolf packs up north," Dani says. "There's that inbred group in Alberta, and the one in northern Manitoba that's always ripping apart the newest alpha male during the full moon. Oh, and—"

"I know! I know! I can fantasize about a werewolf-free Canada, can't I?"

Dani sighs. "I guess if I can imagine Evan buying me doughnuts, you can have a supernatural-free Canada."

The bell rings, and we uncloak and head out.

"Hey, what are we going to get Margo for her birthday?" I ask.

"I know what I want to get her."

"What?"

Dani looks around, and then whispers in my ear. "A spell to remove the stick from her ass."

I stifle a laugh—and look around, too—hating that I'm afraid of Margo sneaking up on us. "I'm dreading the meeting this weekend. It figures Margo turns eighteen first. She's bad enough as it is—once she's part of the inner circle, she'll be insufferable."

"Look," Dani says, pointing down the hall. "There's Connor."

I follow her hand and meet Connor's eyes. Goose bumps run up my arm as I wave to him. He turns away, and continues walking down the hall.

"I don't think he saw you," Dani says softly.

My stomach does a slow, uneasy turn as my blood turns cold. "Yeah, I guess he didn't," I say, but I know it's a lie. I'm thinking I'm the biggest idiot in the world for listening to Connor last night—for doing what we did.

But maybe I was wrong. Maybe he didn't see me.

"Hey, Jules! Dani, wait up!"

We turn around and Michael comes puffing up to us. "What's the matter, ladies? You two look like you couldn't conjure up a pair of glass slippers with a fairy Godmother's wand."

I roll my eyes. "That's so lame."

"Sorry," Michael says. "Growing up sheltered in an enclave of witches has limited my exposure to real humor. And let me tell you, the guy's locker room isn't a much better source. At least not in mixed company."

"We were just trying to think of what to get Margo for her

birthday," I say, scanning the hall to see if Connor will come back.

"Ah, yes, the she-devil comes of age," Michael says, waggling his eyebrows. "And Saturday she gets to go where no male coven member will ever set foot—Mrs. Keyes' inner sanctum to learn the dark secrets of the coven. Mwha-ha-ha!"

"Aw, you guys get no respect," Dani says.

"Damn straight we don't! We track the haunts down, we liquor them up, promise them all sorts of unspeakable things, and then we get to be the coven garbage men, cleaning up the mess after you ice them."

Dani shakes her head. "Not with the vampires. They just turn to dust, so there's really nothing to clean up after."

Michael and I look at each other, and shake our heads. "*We know*," we say together.

"Seriously," Michael says, "if I were you, I'd skip the presents for Margo, and arm yourselves with bitch-repellent because after Saturday she's gonna ride your asses like a broomstick through a hurricane."

I nod. "That's what we're afraid of."

"Hey, Connor wanted me to give you this," Michael says, reaching into his coat pocket. He pulls out a piece of paper folded into a two-inch square. I take it and try to keep my hand from shaking.

"Uh, thanks."

I let Dani and Michael walk ahead of me as I unfold the note.

We need to talk—

Connor

Shit.

4

Dani stretches out on my bed, and leans over my
night table, reaching for a handful of pretzels. "So, any luck
getting through to Connor?"

"No. For someone who thinks we need to talk, he's doing a
damned good job avoiding me." I look at myself in the mirror,
and realize I'm way overdressed for a coven meeting, even if we
are "celebrating" Margo's birthday and initiation.

"He's probably just scared. I mean if his mom found out
you guys were messing around, who knows what she might
have said to him? Can't you just picture it—Helena looking
up at him with her beady little eyes, 'Darling, if you so much
as touch that girl again, I will magically shrink your balls until
they look more like raisins than testicles.'"

"Oh, my God, Dani!"

"What?"

"What you just said!"

Dani rolls her eyes. "Well, maybe I'm not the goody-goody everyone thinks I am! And tell me you couldn't picture Helena saying that."

"OK, actually I could, but Connor said he'd do everything possible to make sure we'd be together. He said he'd stand up to her if he had to." I sigh. "Of course, that was *before* I got half naked." I take off my sapphire earrings, and pull the black cashmere sweater over my head, and hang it back up. "I don't know what to wear."

"Who cares?" Dani says through a mouthful of pretzels. "This is Margo's big night, no one will be looking at us."

I turn and give her a "do I have to spell it out for you" look.

"Oh, Connor," she says nodding. "What are you so worried about? He never cared what you looked like before."

I give her another look. "Thanks—not that I really care what he thinks anymore."

"Oh, you've been agonizing over what shirt to wear for the last hour for my sake?" She bites down on another pretzel, and shakes her head. "But you know what I mean—Sascha's got the regal-freaking-gorgeous hair thing, and Z's got the hard-ass-exotic Amazon look—I have no clue what Margo's got, beside a pointy face and a bad case of the bitches, but

Connor's always been into plain old you. Uh, not that you're plain."

"I think I felt better before you tried to cheer me up." I grab the sweatshirt I wore two nights ago off the floor and bring it to my face, breathing in Connor's sandalwood aftershave.

"You're not going to wear that, are you? It was on the floor."

I throw the sweatshirt into my empty laundry basket and take out my purple wool sweater—not too fancy, but not too casual. "How about this?"

Dani nods. "Perfect. Margo hates purple."

I put the sweater on and run my fingers through my curls to tame the static. "Do you think Margo will like our presents?"

"I'm still iffy on the book."

"As Margo likes to say, 'it's just a joke.' Anyway, let's pack it all up and get something to eat before the meeting." I sit at my desk and open the black gift bag we bought, and hand it to Dani. "One bar of lavender soap, lavender oil, and lavender lotion—for *improved mood*."

Dani takes each one, wraps them in pink tissue paper, and drops them in the bag.

"One copy of *The Crucible*."

Dani grabs the book and laughs. "It is kind of funny," she says, wrapping it up. "At least she'll like the necklace—I think."

"She'll like it," I say, holding the silver star necklace up.

The opal in the middle flickers with color as it swings from my hand. Dani and I bought a necklace for each of us to celebrate our upcoming birthdays, and to try to recapture some sort of cohesiveness in the group. Not that I really believe matching necklaces will turn us back to the tight-knit group we used to be, but who knows?

"What does the card say about opals?" Dani asks.

I take the small card out of the box and open it up. "'The opal, October's birthstone, is thought to contain captured lightning. Opals bring the wearer inner beauty, success, and facilitate the abilities of foresight and prophecy.'"

"Well, Margo could sure use a dose of inner beauty. What does mine say?"

I take out the boxes with Dani and Zahara's names on them. "'The topaz, November's birthstone, protects the wearer against enemies, untimely death, and is a symbol of beauty and splendor.'"

Dani gets up and takes her box. "You know—with all the night calls we've been going on lately, I think I'm going to put mine on now."

"It's supposed to be for your birthday!"

Dani sticks her tongue out and snatches her necklace out of the box before I can pull it away. She fastens the clasp and looks at herself in my mirror. "Why don't we give them all out tonight?"

"I guess we could. It'll steal a bit of the spotlight away from Margo." I take my necklace out of the box and rub my fingers on the blue stone. "Mine says 'Turquoise, December's birthstone, protects the wearer from evil, and warns of approaching danger.' Do you really think the stones do what the cards say?"

"Do you believe in witches?" Dani says with a laugh.

"Ha-ha, but seriously—stones and crystals are so Wiccan, and most of that stuff is nonsense and luck, right?"

Dani shrugs. "Let's ask your mom."

"Gemstones in themselves are just vessels for power," Mom says. "They need to be activated to be useful."

"Why don't we ever use them, then?" I ask.

Mom puts the necklaces back in their boxes and pushes them across the kitchen table toward Dani and me. "Oh, it's a bother. You need blood to activate them, and the duration of the power is unpredictable. A person might head out not knowing their vessel had emptied—so to speak. Then they confront someone or something, thinking they're protected and I'm sure you can imagine the unpleasant results."

We both nod.

Mom gets up and I can't help but roll my eyes. She's wearing her lame initiation robe embroidered with moons and stars, and a hideous crocheted silver scarf wrapped around

44

her neck. After I go through my initiation, the first thing I'm going to do is petition to do away with the moronic ceremonial uniforms.

"Well, I better head out—I told Helena I'd help set things up," Mom says. "Don't wait up for me after you get home." She takes her dress cape out of the closet, and grabs her broom.

"How long does it take to say 'Happy birthday, welcome to the club?'"

Mom looks at me like I'm three again. "It's a bit more involved than that, though I'm sure with Margo, things will run smoothly."

"Are you implying my initiation won't go smoothly?"

Mom winks. "That all depends on you."

"We'll see you soon, Mrs. Harris," Dani says. "We're gonna grab something to eat, and then we'll fly over."

"Don't be late, girls."

Mom heads out the door and I look at the necklaces on the table. "Let's do it!"

"What? Nachos?"

"No! Let's activate the stones."

Dani curls her lip and shakes her head. "Uh, no. I don't like spells that need blood. It's bad enough getting scratched or bit when we're hunting, but drawing blood on purpose? I'll pass."

"Fine, we'll use my blood."

"We don't even know how to activate the stones."

"That's what books are for."

Dani looks at her watch. "We have to be at the meeting-house in, like, forty minutes and I'm hungry."

I get up and pull a couple of books off the shelf in the living room and bring them into the kitchen. "If we can't find a spell soon we'll skip it, okay?"

Dani reaches out for a red leather book titled *Birth Signs, Stones, and Spells* and opens to the table of contents. "I guess." She looks down at the page, and sighs. "'Chapter seven, page forty-six—activating birthstones.'" She flips through the book and shrugs her shoulders. "Actually, this doesn't look too bad. We need to write down all of our birthdays on separate slips of parchment, wrap the necklaces in them, put them in a bowl with five drops of blood, and set them on fire. When the paper burns off, the stones will be activated."

"Cool! I'll get Mom's spell bowl from the pantry. You cut up some paper, and I'll write our birthdays down."

I take the first piece of paper. "Margo—October twenty-fifth. Sascha—October twenty-ninth. Dani—November first. Zahara—November tenth. Julia—December third."

"I want to wrap mine up," Dani says.

We put the wrapped necklaces in the bowl, and Dani hands me a pin. "You sure about this?"

I look at the tip of my finger and jab it in. "Ow, yeah." I squeeze out five drops of blood, landing one on each packet. Dani lights a match and drops it in the bowl. We jump back as fire shoots up two feet in air.

"Holy shit!" Dani yells. "That almost burned my bangs off!"

We watch the fire devour the parchment paper, and then I fish out the necklaces by hooking the pin in the chains.

Dani gingerly pokes hers. "Wow, it's cold."

I pick my necklace up and rub the turquoise. "Evil beware," I say, fastening the clasp.

Dani puts hers on. "I feel safer already."

"Let's pack up the other necklaces and head out—if we hurry we can give them to everyone before Margo's birthday candle is lit."

Dani elbows me, and rolls her eyes when Helena calls Margo up to the front of the room. Helena's piled her white hair up in some sort of weird tangle—more bird's nest than bun, and with her silver dress robe and scarf, she looks like a ghost about to disappear into a gray mist.

Helena nods and Margo's mom joins them at the front of the room, taking Margo's hand in hers. Her dad waves from the side of the room, and I remember how Margo used to lord it over us that she and Zahara were the only ones whose fathers were still around—as if that made them better than the rest of us.

I look at Sascha on my other side playing with the chain of her necklace. She turns and smiles at me. "Thanks again—it's really cool," she whispers.

Zahara leans forward and glares at us. "Shh!"

I look around the room, only one chair empty out of thirty-five. Everyone's here except Connor.

"Tonight," Helena begins, "we welcome Margo into our inner circle. I know I speak for all of us when I say we couldn't be happier our girls are now coming of age, and ready to embrace their new roles in the coven."

She nods her head at Dani, Sascha, Zahara, and me. I plaster a smile on my face and wish she'd just get on with it so I can head home and check my cell messages to see if Connor called.

"Let us start with Margo's birthday candle." She places a small black stub of a candle on the silver cloth covering the table.

Margo strikes a match and lights the candle.

"For eighteen years we've lit this candle as a symbol of Margo's journey toward becoming a full member of our Revealer Sisterhood. Tonight, when the wick burns away the last bit of wax, Margo will join the inner circle and finally know her destiny."

We all clap, and Hattie Murphy, the coven accountant, turns in her seat and looks at us with tears in her eyes. "No worries, girls. Everything will be fine."

"Hattie!" snaps Margo's grandmother, Miranda, who's sitting next to her. She turns and smiles at us. And waves a shaking hand dismissively. She's so thin and frail, I find it hard to picture those shaky hands of hers ever spiking a vamp.

Miranda smiles broader and her faded blue eyes are lost in the crinkles. "Of course, everything will be fine. This is a wonderful time for you girls." She faces the front again, but I don't miss the fact that she kicks Hattie ever so slightly with the side of her foot.

"Like the generations of Revealers who have come before us," Helena continues, "Margo will become a part of the coven's guiding hand that is sworn to protect mankind from the monsters that haunt us."

Helena wraps an ugly silver scarf around Margo's neck, kisses her on the cheeks, and faces us smiling. A chill runs up the back of my neck. Helena's smiles have never seemed right to me— like she's smiling, but she'd really rather be biting our heads off.

"We've watched Margo grow from a child into a strong, determined young woman who I know will continue to be an asset to the coven. Margo demonstrates poise beyond her years, and I am confident she will carry the mantle of responsibility well."

Margo throws her shoulders back and looks out at us. All I can think is she's taking this way too seriously, but then she's always been really into all the coven crap. She reaches up, fingers her star necklace, and blinks twice. She takes in a sharp breath and looks around the room, with wide eyes. I swear I see her opal crackle with light—like the "captured lightning" is trying to escape. Margo pales and drops the necklace under her robe. She turns her head to Helena and then her mother—brow furrowed.

Sascha leans in toward me. "Did you see that?"

"The necklace?" I ask.

"Yeah."

Sascha holds her star up by its chain—the opal is flickering, but nothing like Margo's. She moves her eyebrows up and down. "Freaky!"

I try to remember what the card said about opals. *Inner beauty? Foresight?*

I look down at the star resting on my chest. The gem in the middle is glowing blue and I cover it with my hands. Am I being warned of approaching danger, or guarded from evil? I scan the room and look at the familiar faces I've grown up with. Everyone's eyes are on Margo, nothing seems wrong. The door in the back opens slowly and Connor slinks in. My cheeks flush and I turn my focus back up front.

I realize Helena's asked everyone to come forward and congratulate Margo before they take her away for the private part of the ceremony. I get in the line and nearly pass out when Connor slides in behind me and presses his chest against my back.

He puts a hand on my shoulder and leans in closer—his warm breath burning my neck. "Meet me at your mom's studio," he whispers, sending goose bumps up my arms. "So we can talk."

"Uh—" I stammer, but he's already gone—winding his way through the crowd to the door.

"What did he want?" Dani asks.

"To meet me at my house."

"That's good, right?" Dani asks.

I bite my lip. "Too soon to say."

Dani squeezes my hand. "You'll work it out, I know it."

I make it to the front of the line, and give Margo a weak hug. "Your necklace was flashing—did you see it?"

Margo looks past me to Dani. "It—it was nothing." She holds out a hand to Dani—I've been dismissed.

Dani meets me outside. "Is your necklace doing anything?" I ask.

"Actually, it was kind of bumping around just before." She pulls the chain out from her cape. "Oh, my God."

The star is jerking around—the inside of the topaz swirling, like it's filled with a yellow fog being whipped around in a storm.

I lift my star up. "Look at mine."

"What does it mean?" she asks.

"Maybe it's a sign that Connor's going to break up with me."

"Or maybe it's a sign that something bad is going down."

I drop the star under my cape and shake my head. "I bet we end up going on a hunt tonight, that's got to be it."

"Yeah."

Dani and I stand in silence, and I wish I wasn't filled with a deep sense of dread. "Well, I better get going—not that I'm in any rush to get dumped."

Dani squeezes my hand. "He's not going to dump you, but if he does, I'll research the nuts-to-raisins spell myself!"

"I can think of at least one other thing that might need to be shrunk!"

Dani laughs. "Call me as soon as you can."

"Okay." I mount my broom and head home. The wind freezes my cheeks and hands—I will it to freeze my heart so I won't be able to feel a thing if Connor decides to break it.

5

I uncloak as I land in my yard, and stumble none-
too-gracefully to a stop. It's hard to land smoothly when your
feet are numb. I try to tread quietly through the frosty leaves,
lean my broom gently on a nearby tree, and peek in the front
window of Mom's shop—the pale yellow flicker of candles
inside warming the glass.

My insides melt when I see three small, white jack-o'-
lanterns—Luminas—lined up against the far window by the
pond. The light from the candles catches in the glass strands
of the witch balls hanging above them. A *C* is carved in the
first pumpkin, a heart in the second, and a crooked *J* carved in
the third. There's a small red candle on the table next to one
long-stemmed white rose, and Connor is looking nervously at
the door.

I watch him and smile, knowing he remembered that every Halloween I always pick white pumpkins instead of the plain orange ones. Madeline Kline, who cultivates the small field near the coven meeting house, always plants a special row of Luminas and Baby Boos just for me. She told me a while back that the cool spring rain damaged a lot of the pumpkins and my white ones didn't make it this year. So that means Connor went out of his way to find these.

It means he does still care.

He takes his wallet out and lays it on the table in front of him. We didn't have condoms last time—did he buy some? Are they in his leather wallet? Is that why he said he wanted to meet? So we could finish what we didn't last time?

I frown and feel a wave of anger bubble up in me, bursting any hope I had for this evening. If Connor thinks carving our initials in a few gourds is going to make up for the fact that he blew me off after our first heavy hook up—after all the things he said and promised—well, he has another thing coming.

I open the door and put my hands on my hips. "So, you're finally ready to talk?" I say in my coldest voice. I don't move toward him and almost smirk when his brow furrows.

"Yeah, Jules." He stands up. "I'm sorry," he says with a pained look.

"Oh, about what?"

"Jules, you know."

I stare at him waiting for him to go on—to tell me he was a jerk or scared or something to make up for the fact that I trusted him so completely, and then he bailed on me. When he doesn't say anything, I roll my eyes. "Well, I guess we're done here—apology not accepted."

I turn to leave and he rushes toward me and touches my arm. "Wait, this isn't easy for me. I—I know I should've called you, and I know you were probably wondering what was going on and . . ."

"Damn straight I was wondering what was going on!" I say, pulling my arm away from him. "God, Connor, you told me you loved me, we almost went all the way, and then you act like I don't exist. I know you saw me in the hall at school. And then to top it all off, you have Michael give me a note like we're ten or something. Not that you even meant what you said in your stupid four-word note. I called you five times before I decided I was making a complete ass out of myself!"

He grabs my hand and pulls me close. "You don't understand," he says. "My mom was waiting for me, she knew."

He's still holding my hand, and part of me knows what facing his mom must have been like—I can picture her steely eyes boring into his, but he said he'd fight for me, and it's obvious he gave up without even trying. "You told me it didn't matter what your mother thought." I try to yank away from him but he holds on tight, so I turn away and look at the stupid pumpkins. "I'm such an idiot to have bought into all your bullshit!"

Tears sting my eyes as the effort it's taken to stay strong and pretend Connor doesn't matter these last two days dissolves. "I am such an idiot," I choke out, feeling my legs buckle.

He comes up behind me and I'm too tired to fight him.

"Jules, I'm the idiot, not you. I'm sorry I put you through this. Please just stay and hear me out, okay?"

I stared at the jagged heart he carved in the middle pumpkin. "Whatever." I let him lead me reluctantly to the couch.

"My mom was waiting for me; she knew. I don't know how, some sort of witch thing maybe, but I opened the door and she up and slapped me. My own mother—no warning, and then she was raging at me, and she may not look like much, but it was like getting hit by a demon."

"Like you'd know what that felt like."

Connor glares at me. "Sorry I wasn't born with special powers and don't get to go at it with demons on a regular basis."

I look up at him and see fear and sadness in his blue eyes. I hold my hand up to his face and whisper, "*Reveal.*" A small pink handprint rises on his cheek, and I bite my lip. "Oh, Connor," I say, bringing my hand up to cover the mark. "I should've realized. I mean I thought this all might have been because of your mom, but I was so upset and then I got mad. But you should've come to me."

He covers my hand with his, presses it to his face, and then takes it to his lips and kisses it, making my heart flutter. "You don't know how badly I wanted to tell you, but she was crazy. She said all these things, and I—I didn't know what to do. I needed time to figure things out, to think how we could be together when you're a hunter with all the rules and stupid freaking traditions that go with it." He drops my hand and drops his chin to his chest. "And I'm just a nothing, whose grand purpose in life is cleaning up roadkill."

"No, it's not like that—"

Connor shakes his head. "Jules, you just as much said it yourself a minute ago. You can pretend all you want that I'm destined for something bigger, but it is what it is. I'm a guy riding the coattails of a bunch of monster-hunting witches." He stands up and walks to the witch balls hanging on the curtain rod. He twists one, winding the string tight, then lets it go, sending the ball into a frantic spin. "You women have been holding all the power since the 1600s when the coven was first approached, I, uh—" He stops the ball with his hand. "I mean, was *formed*, and us guys have just been along for the ride ever since."

I get up and wrap my arms around him, pressing my chest into his back. I rest my head on his shoulder blade and sigh.

"It's the twenty-first century, you can be whatever you want—
we can be whatever we want."

"I don't know anymore," he says quietly. "But we'd both
be lying if we said that making a change in the coven would
be easy. You know what we're up against, and as much as I
wanted to think it would be easy to make all the roadblocks
disappear, it's not going to happen. My mother won't let it.
There's too much at stake."

He sighs and I hug him tighter. "Let's just be together for
now." I reach around for his hand and we sit on the couch.
"Where'd you get the pumpkins?"

Connor smiles. "Seeing as I'm as magical as a can of worms,
I called a bunch of farms until I found one that was growing
the white ones. I remembered how much you like them, and
Ms. Kline said hers didn't come up this year."

"That was really sweet," I say, and then lean in and gently
kiss him on the lips.

"I got you something else," he says, reaching for his
wallet.

My heart beats faster wondering if tonight *will* be the
night.

He opens it up and pulls out a tiny manila envelope instead of a pack of condoms from behind some bills. Relief and
a bit of disappointment flush through me, but I figure after
what's happened it's better to take things slowly.

He tips it over his palm, and a silver-and-gold ring slips out and lands in his open hand. "My mom has a room in the house filled with all sorts of old stuff—I think you guys get some of it after kills, and some of it's been around a long time from other hunters, but put it on."

"Wow, this must be the universe's way of telling me I need to accessorize more," I say, feeling giddy Connor is giving me a ring! "I got a new necklace today, too."

I'm about to pull out my necklace to show him, but he takes my right hand and slides the ring on my finger. "It's an Ouroboros," he says. "You know—the symbol of unity and eternity."

My heart quickens. "I've seen this before," I say, looking down at the snake, with its tail in his mouth, loosely coiled around my finger. The head and the top half of the body are gold, the rest silver with ruby eyes that sparkle in the candlelight.

"Oh!" My right hand suddenly starts to quiver. "We got this off a demon we killed in ninth grade! Your mother told us not to come home without it." I start to pull it off, but the snake lets out a soft hiss, and I yank my hand away like I've been bitten. The head starts to move and gulp the tail down its throat, until the ring fits tightly around my finger. "Oh, my God, Connor!" I say, shaking my hand—trying to dislodge the ring. "What the hell is happening?"

Connor jumps up, his eyes wide. "I don't know! There was a paper in the box, it didn't say the ring moved or anything, just that the eyes are supposed to glow if—"

"If what?"

"If the person who gave it to you is telling the truth. I swear I didn't know it moved or anything."

"Well, it did! The freaking ring swallowed its own tail," I say, holding my shaking hand far from my body. I hold my left hand over it. "*Remove!*" I say. The spell swirls around my hand, but the snake just wiggles, takes another gulp, and the ring cuts deeper into my finger. "Ow!" My legs start to shake, and I flop down on the couch. "What if it's cursed? Did you research the thing? And what if your mom finds out it's missing?"

Connor puts his hands out to calm me down. "No, no—don't worry. It's okay. From what I read, the ring lets you know when the person who gave it to you is telling the truth. That's it. I just wanted you to be able to trust me. I just wanted to talk to you and then I was going to put it back."

I stare at the snake's head, my heart pounding wildly. "What else did it say?"

"Not much, just something like it was—uh, well, demon in origin, and—"

"Well, that's not a huge surprise," I say bitterly, "seeing as we got it off a demon! We had to cut its finger off to get the ring, you know."

I wince thinking about the sound of Margo's knife sawing through the bone—the blackish-blue demon blood sizzling on the pavement. I remember Dani saying she saw the ring move, but we all thought she was crazy.

I guess I owe her an apology.

I touch the ring and when it doesn't move, try to pull it off. It hisses and I let it go, not wanting it to strangle my finger again.

"It's stuck and when I try to pull it off, it just hangs on tighter!" I throw my head back onto the back of the couch feeling exhausted. "For future reference, Connor, jewelry forged in hell is not on my top ten list of gifts I'm hoping for." I take a deep breath and will my heartbeats to return to normal.

"I'm so, so sorry, Jules, I didn't think it mattered where it'd come from, and I was kind of hoping you wouldn't ask." He closes his eyes and sighs. "I guess I didn't think beyond the fact that this would let you know I was telling you the truth. So you'd know I was really sorry. That I do love you."

The Ouroboros's eyes glow stronger, and its mouth moves, releasing a bit of the tail and loosening its tight grasp.

"Look at that! See," he says, pointing at the ring.

I hold my hand in front of my face and shake my head. "Oh, well, I guess this makes wearing a demonic ring okay then. Who cares that the snake came to life and swallowed its tail to magically attach itself to my hand, and the only way to remove it may be by hacking it off? I'm sure Margo is just itching to try amputating another finger."

"This isn't exactly going the way I'd planned."

"You think?"

"Jules, look at me." Connor gently places his hand on my face and turns it toward him. His touch sends a jolt of electricity coursing down my spine. "I got scared after talking to my mom—really scared—and I was a complete jerk for not telling you right away, but I really am sorry."

The snake's eyes pulse with red light, and despite the fact that my heart is still beating a mile a minute, I can't help but feel relieved.

"I guess there's probably some spell to get rings off," I say. "I can go through some of my mom's books." I look at Connor. "So what all did your mother say to you?" I ask, leaning my shoulder into his. "The girls need to wait until the right time—it's all got to be coordinated—we can't have any unexpected pregnancies, blah, blah, blah."

"Yeah," he says, "the same old stuff, but she was harping on and on about the coven's mission, and how fooling around with you could mess that up and stuff."

The snake's eyes pulse. "Well, that's nothing to get all freaked out about—we've been fed that line forever, right?"

Connor doesn't say anything, and we sit in silence. The

candle in the center pumpkin starts to sputter and burns out. I watch a thin trail of smoke leak out of the heart. I point my hand toward the hole. *"Relight."* A new wick appears and bursts into a tall flame that licks the top of the pumpkin. I smell the burning flesh and whisper, *"Lower."* The flame settles down to a tiny flicker and I look up at Connor. "Did she say anything else?"

"She was just really freaked out that you aren't taking things as seriously as you should," he finally says, "and she said dating would only make things worse."

"Why did she single me out? What about Dani? What about Sascha? It's not like they're all gung-ho like Margo and Z."

"I wasn't fooling around with Dani or Sascha, I was with you. Look, bottom line is my mom takes this way seriously."

"Ha, tell me about it!"

"And, in a way, she's right."

"What?" I sit up, eyebrows raised.

"It's just that people need you, and what you do. Just think of what the world would be like if you weren't—"

"What? Slicing and dicing nightmares? God, you sound like a greeting card—or one of our mothers!"

"Come on, Jules, don't you feel a little bit, you know, proud of what you do?"

"I don't know—maybe. But I'm beginning to wonder if

your mother cast a spell to brainwash you into buying into the coven crap."

Connor pulls me close and buries his face into my neck leaving a trail of kisses until he reaches my mouth. He lingers there, and I kiss him back until he pulls away. "Would I be doing this if I was buying into it all?" he whispers.

"No." I smile and kiss him again. "But where does this leave us—sneaking around?" I stand up and walk to the pumpkins. I want him to tell me he got scared, but now he's ready to fight—but I know that's not how this is going down. He wouldn't have brought the ring if he were ready to battle. This ring is to placate me for the time being.

"Just for a little while. Until everything settles down—until my mom cools off. Don't you think it's better than the alternative?"

"I guess," I lie, wanting him to stand up to his mother for me. I wave my hand in front of the pumpkins. "*Out,*" I say, and the candles extinguish at the same time. I turn toward the table and point to the small candle on the table. "*You, too.*" A small puff of air blows by, snuffing out the candle. I stand there in the dark, my back to Connor, breathing in the smoke. What do I do? Concede things aren't easy to change? Now isn't the right time to change the way the coven's been doing things the last couple of hundred years?

But if we continue—what's to keep his mom, or my mom

for that matter, from finding out? I'm sure Helena's put my mom on alert.

"Are you willing to risk pissing off your mom to be with me?" I hold my right hand out and wait.

"We just need to be smart about this, plan things out. Like tonight she'll be too wrapped up in Margo's initiation to worry about me. And as long as you're pretending to be the coven's number one hunter, she won't be worrying about you, either."

"What if I don't want to pretend? What if I want us to be together where everyone will see us?"

Connor comes up behind me, brushes my hair aside, and kisses the nape of my neck. He presses his hips into me, and my heart quickens. "It's just for a little while, Jules, and after your birthday you'll have more say about how things are run." He wraps his arms around me, pulling me close, and then slides one hand under my shirt. His cool hand runs across my stomach, and then skims down just under my waistband, making my knees weak. "I promise we *will* find a way to work this out."

The red eyes glow bright and steady in the dark, and I exhale. "Okay, we'll play it your way—for a little while, but only because I don't think I can stand being away from you again. Promise me you'll come to me next time. Promise me you won't leave me hanging like that."

I face Connor, his features muted in the dark.

"I promise," he says, leaning in to kiss me.

I hold my right hand up behind him and watch the red eyes glow, and then I close my own eyes and let myself go.

I lift my head up at the sound of "Danse Macabre." Dani and I thought it would be a funny ring tone, but right now it's a definite mood killer. "Oh, shit, I better get that," I say, pushing off of Connor.

Breathless, I fish my phone out of my cape pocket. I look at the caller ID and just about die. "It's your mother!" I grab my shirt from the table and pull it over my head before I answer.

"Hi, Mrs. Keyes," I say, trying very hard to make my voice sound normal. "Vamp? Okay. The meeting is for eleven thirty— yeah, I can be there before then. Do you need me to call anyone? Do they have binders? Okay, I'll head right over!"

I click the phone off. "Well, here's my chance to be the best darn slayer this coven has ever seen. Did you hear me asking about binders? Did I sound enthusiastic enough?" I raise my hands to the witch balls. "Light."

Connor sits up on the couch and brushes his hair out of his eyes. "Did I say you should be the coven's number one hunter?" He reaches out and pulls me down on top of him. "I changed my mind!"

I giggle as he starts tugging my shirt up. "Hey, out-slaying Margo and Z was your brilliant plan." I give him a quick kiss, and then get up and look around on the floor for my bra.

"Fine," he says, sitting up. "But who knows when we'll be able to sneak away again?"

"That's no longer my concern, because until this particular member of the undead tastes the pointed wrath of the Revealers, I have no time for earthly pleasures!" I pull my arms out of my shirt and slide my bra on.

Connor laughs. "Yeah, better take that act down a notch, or they'll know something's up for sure. But since it's a vamp, I'm off the hook for tonight." He buttons his shirt and sighs. "Although, if I had to be on cleanup crew I could at least steal another good-night kiss. I guess I'll have to steal one now."

He grabs me and kisses me hard. "And let me help you with this." He hooks the back of my bra while nibbling on the base of my neck. I run my hands across his bare shoulders, and I'm tempted to blow off the whole hunt, but then I think about impressing his mom.

"Enough!" I say, and push him away. "I have evil to vanquish!" I laugh as I stick my arms back through my sleeves, and grab my cape off the arm of the sofa.

Connor raises his eyebrows and shakes his head.

"Yeah, I know—bring it down a notch."

Connor runs his hands through his hair again and then

adjusts his pants. "I guess I'll go home and take a cold shower. If I'm lucky I can get in bed before my mom gets home."

I look at the disheveled couch cushions, the candle stub on the table, and the pumpkins—hating what I'm about to say. "Hey, I really don't like the thought of zapping the cute pumpkins you carved into oblivion with a spell. Do you think you could maybe clean up a little so my mom doesn't know we were out here? I'd do it, but the new me shouldn't be the last one to arrive."

"Sure, cleanup crew is my middle name."

He smiles, but I can't help feeling guilty. "Forget it, I'll do it when I get back—I'll have time to go out in the morning before she gets to work—she always sleeps in."

Connor walks over and kisses me. "I'm just yanking your chain. I don't mind, and the less evidence we leave behind, the better. Now get going!" He slaps me on the ass and I head out.

I take my broom and run over to the mudroom door by the kitchen. Nuisance comes trotting out, and I quickly rub the top of his head. "Gotta go, baby," I coo, heading in. I walk over to the old chest and flip open the top. I check out a couple stakes, choose pine, and slip it in my cloak. I grab a maple one for backup, and plunge it in the air as I run back outside. "*Hasta la vista*, vamp."

I slip the stake in my other pocket and mount my broom.

"I fly in darkness for the good of all, let me pass unseen till I land again." The electric tingle of the cloaking spell rushes over me and I head up over the trees toward the high school, hoping the vamp goes down quickly so I can go back home and dream about Connor.

6

I land behind the baseball dugout, and wonder if I'm the first one. Dragging my broom through the dirt, I walk to the front and see Zahara, Sascha, and Dani sitting silently on the bench—a small fluorescent lightbulb crackles on and off above them.

"No Margo yet? Where is she?" I ask, pleased she'll be the last to arrive for a change.

"I'm not sure. She was at the meetinghouse when they got the call, so she should be here soon," Zahara says quietly.

"Well, after the crap she gave me about my mom not seeing the stupid cauldron she should—"

"Jules," Dani interrupts, "it's Kelsey DeFelice. That's who we're after tonight."

I bite my lip, hating myself for joking about tonight's kill with Connor earlier. I didn't think it'd be someone I know—someone my age. We haven't hunted anyone we knew in years, and just the thought of staking Kelsey makes my stomach turn. "I thought she'd just dropped out of school. When did they get her?"

"Apparently she wanted to take the goth stuff to the next level and got herself turned on purpose," Zahara says. "At least that's what Mrs. Keyes told my mom."

"Why would anyone do that? That's crazy—that's a . . ."

"A death wish," Sascha says. "God, this sucks—I like Kelsey. She was one of the few girls at school who actually talked to me. She was my partner for the pig dissection in ninth grade. We named our pig Lucifer, and I did all of the cutting because, ironically, she was too grossed out. We used to drink peppermint schnapps in the locker room showers before gym class last year." Sascha laughs quietly. "She always said we had to be minty-fresh and buzzed so we could deal with the jock girls and floor hockey."

Zahara lowers her chin and shakes her head. "My mom said she's turned a bunch of guys since she got bit. We have to do it—she's a killing machine—like all the rest of them. And if she got herself turned she knew the risks. It's not like vamps think they're untouchable—they know people are out hunting them. We need to treat her like any other vampire—toast!"

"I heard it's like crack," Dani whispers.

"Crack?" Zahara asks. "What the hell are you talking about?"

Dani fidgets with her broom handle. "Online—there's this, like, message board, and well, I don't know if the people on it are really vamps or not, but from what they're saying, getting bit is like—*orgasmic.*"

"Oh, my freaking God!" Zahara says. "Little Miss Innocent is trolling vamp-wannabe message boards reading about orgasms! You didn't believe that bull, did you? Even if they were real vamps on there, they'd just be feeding people what they want to hear so they can sink their fangs in them. Crack!" she laughs. "Wait until Margo hears this."

"I—I, uh, was just doing research," Dani sputters. "I knew it was all made up—I was just telling you what I read. But shouldn't we be getting ready for Kelsey?"

"Yeah, it's almost time," I say, trying to help Dani change the subject. I finger the tip of my stake in my pocket. "Who's gonna bind her?"

"I'll do it," Sascha says. "I've got one in my hand already, but I don't want to dust her."

No one says another word, and I know we're all hoping someone else will volunteer to do it, or that Kelsey will get nasty and one of us won't mind doing the deed. I pull on the chain of my necklace and I'm relieved to see the stone in the center is dark.

"Maybe she won't show up," I say.

"Troy?" a voice calls out.

"That's her," Dani says. "She's coming."

"Andreeeew," Kelsey calls out in a singsong voice.

Her footsteps get closer and I stuff my necklace back under my cape so Kelsey won't see it when it starts to glow. I realize the dugout light is still on and my heart quickens as I look for the switch.

"Out!" Dani says, pointing to the bare bulb, beating me to it.

I breathe a sigh of relief that the parking lot lights don't reach all the way into the benches.

"Where ya hiding, guys?" Kelsey calls out.

"Damn," Sascha whispers. "This sucks."

"You boys ready for me?" Kelsey says as she rounds the corner. "You ready to . . ." She sees us and freezes. "Whoa, Sascha? Is that you? Julia Harris?" She nods at Dani and Z. "You girls partying out here?"

My eyes go wide as I wait for Sascha to throw the binder.

"Hey, Kelsey," Zahara says. "Long time no see! What've you been up to? You got smart and ditched the school thing I heard."

I'm glad Z has the brains to stall for time. I nudge Sascha and think I see a tear glide down her cheek.

"Ha, yeah," Kelsey says. "Somethin' like that." She runs

her fingers through her black hair and hitches up her baggy pants. "You seen Troy Dillon and Andrew White? They graduated last year, but we kinda have a date." Kelsey winks and her black lipsticked mouth beaks into a knowing smile.

"Haven't seen them," Zahara says, "but we were just about to light up a joint—want to join us?"

Kelsey laughs. "Man, I had a feeling those two were gonna blow me off, but so what? I'll party with you girls tonight! Show them, huh?"

She walks into the dugout and I elbow Sascha again. "Let's get going, Sascha. *Light* it up." Sascha's hand bumps into mine, and I realize she's trying to pass the binder to me.

"I see you girls got smart and ditched that bitch, Margo. I never could figure out what you saw in her, Sascha, I mean, damn that girl . . ." Kelsey pauses and looks at each of us each in turn—her eyebrows raised. "What is *up* with the Little Red Riding Hood look? This is obviously some fashion trend I missed, and I'm thinking you shoulda missed out on it, too!"

I grit my teeth and hate that I'm feeling embarrassed to be wearing a cape. I hate that some three-hundred-year-old rule says it's the only thing to go out hunting in. I hate that we're buying into that rule. I grab the binder, and flinging it at Kelsey's feet—a foot or so off. "We bind you to the earth!" I yell, but I'm pretty sure the binder won't take.

"What the hell?" Kelsey's head jerks around as the dirt

and dust of the dugout floor start to twist up her legs. She stares at us for a split second, and then bares her sharp teeth. "Witches!" She leaps up, morphs into a large brown bat, and flaps against the ceiling of the dugout, then heads toward the wide opening. A small sandstorm rises up trying to capture her before falling back to the ground.

"Reveal!" We scream together, our arms held high, aiming at the bat.

The spell hits, and Kelsey, human again, crashes to the ground on her back just outside the dugout. Sascha throws another binder at her. "We bind you to the earth!"

As Kelsey struggles to get up, the dirt rises up, engulfing her, twisting along her arms and legs and across her stomach—pinning her down. She cranes her head up, looking at us. "What the fuck are you doing to me?"

"I'm sorry," Sascha says. "I didn't want to do this."

Kelsey struggles to move, but the binder's too strong. "You're a fucking witch! Shit! Why didn't you tell me?"

"I—I'm so sorry," Sascha says again. She looks at me and her shoulders cave. "I can't do this." She runs back toward the benches and I hear her sobbing.

"I wasn't gonna get you!" Kelsey spits out. "I just thought we were gonna have a smoke. I wasn't even gonna tell you what I was, 'cause we're friends. Right, Sascha? Sascha! We're friends!" She thrashes around for a few seconds then growls in frustration. "Let me go, okay? You'll never see me again."

Bile rises in my throat as I watch her splayed out on the ground struggling, helpless. I think about all the vamps I've staked without thought—without really, truly caring about who they used to be.

"We can't let you go," I say, keeping my voice steady. "You've hurt too many people."

"Oh, for God's sake! I didn't do anyone that didn't want it. Hell, Troy and Andrew know what I am—we were just gonna have a little fun. I wasn't gonna turn them! Please." Her voice cracks and she starts to cry. "Sascha? Sascha, don't let them do this, please!"

"Look, we're all sorry, but you chose this—you knew the risks," Zahara says, acting the hard-ass again, but I notice she hasn't taken a stake out of her cloak.

"Oh, man, you sanctimonious shits are too much. But even if you bitches go through with this, it'll have been worth it. No regrets!" Kelsey struggles and cranes her neck up off the ground. The binder pulls on her and she throws her head back to the ground, and sighs. "Well, what the hell are you waiting for? You always torture your vics before you kill them? Is that what you sadistic freaks like?"

"No!" I say. "We don't want to do this, but—"

"What's a matter, Sascha, why ya hiding back there? Don't you wanna stake me? Ya gonna let your prissy friend, Zahara, do it? Or what about you, Dani?" she snarls. "Show me how tough you are!"

"Will someone do it already?!" Sascha yells.

Dani looks at me with pleading eyes, but I shake my head. "Z?"

"Why me?" Zahara mutters as she finally pulls a stake out of her cape pocket. "I wish I didn't have to do this, Kelsey, but—"

"Oh, for God's sake," Margo says, landing by home plate. She stalks toward us with one hand on her hip, dragging her broom with the other. "She's still alive?" She stands next to Kelsey, glaring at us all. "You couldn't handle one stupid vamp without me?"

Margo drops her broom, pulls a stake out, and kneels down next to Kelsey. Kelsey's eyes go wide, like she figured none of us would actually go through with it, but now she knows it's really going to happen.

"Margo, no!" Kelsey screams, trying to twist out of the binding. "Please! Let's talk—let's—"

Margo puts one hand on Kelsey's upper chest and then slams the stake into her heart with the other. I hear the stake splinter as it goes through her and hit the ground. Margo turns her head as Kelsey implodes—her last cry echoing in our ears.

Margo stands up and brushes the fine dust—the last

remnants of Kelsey—off the front of her shirt. "What was the problem here? You had her bound—why didn't you stake her?"

Zahara takes a step toward her. "It was *Kelsey*—and you know—we know her and . . ."

"I don't remember anyone complaining when we staked that librarian who used to do story time," Margo says.

"That was different!" I say, amazed Margo is being so cold about this. "That was our first hunt and Miss Melissa was out of control—there was a definite kill-or-be-killed thing going on that night. Kelsey didn't even show her fangs until we tried to bind her!"

Margo laughs. "Oh, please. Do you really think Kelsey was going to hang out with you—no fangs involved? It's classic vamp stuff. She was just trying to get close."

Zahara looks at the rest of us. "I don't know—I kind of think she did just want to party with us."

I nod. "And it's not like she could have taken all of us."

Margo rolls her eyes. "It takes seconds—*seconds* for a vamp to mesmerize someone—or a group of someones. She was obviously going to try to get you under sway, and then take her pick. And what would've prevented her from calling in some friends to help her finish you all off? She was a vamp; we kill vamps. End of discussion."

"But I don't think she was after us—seriously. If you

could've just seen her." Zahara kicks the ground. "Where were you, by the way?"

Margo jerks her head toward Z. "I . . . I was . . . I'm just late, okay?!"

"Fine," Z says, "but don't get on our case if you weren't here to see the whole thing through! And I still say she wasn't going to reveal."

"And you know what?" I add. "My necklace is supposed to warn about danger and it was completely dark seconds before she showed up!"

"Actually," Dani says, "it could've stopped working already. Your mom did say the stones could empty at any time."

Margo takes a deep breath. "Bottom line, this is our job. We can't personalize it."

"Wow, sounds like you got some great insights into hunting during your little initiation," Sascha says, getting up off the bench. She walks right up to Margo—and I can tell Margo's not liking the close proximity.

Sascha tilts her head and looks Margo up and down. "Apparently they exorcised the last remnants of feeling out of you, too."

Margo's mouth drops open, and then she narrows her eyes. "Well, you'll find out soon enough, won't you? Four more days until *your* birthday, and then you can decide for yourself whether or not a vamp's worth crying over."

"I'm out of here," Sascha says, grabbing her broom from the corner of the dugout. "Happy freaking birthday, Margo."

She mounts her broom and heads up, and I stifle the urge to remind her to use the cloaking spell.

"Don't forget to cloak!" Dani yells out.

I shake my head, knowing Dani's going to get shit for that.

Margo turns on Dani immediately, sneering. "God, you just can't keep your mouth shut for a minute, can you? You always have to—"

"Leave her alone," I say, standing between them. "I would've thought you'd be happy she's trying to make sure everyone is doing the right thing—it's what you're always preaching. She just said what we were all thinking!"

Margo curls her lip. "It's the way she says it." She turns toward Dani and scowls. "You think you're the only one who knows everything! You treat us like we're preschoolers just learning about all this shit for the first time, and you don't even know what's really going on!"

"Hey," Zahara says, reaching out a hand on Margo's arm. "Chill out—this was tough enough without all the extra crap. okay?"

Margo folds her hands across her chest and looks down at the ground. She takes a few deep breaths and looks Dani in the eye. "Yeah, I'm sorry. And sorry I was late. I just had a lot to think about." She picks up her stake, sees the point is broken, and chucks it in the garbage can next to the dugout.

Dani shrugs. "It's okay. I do kind of say stuff you already know," she says quietly.

"There, everything's cool, right?" Z says. "Let's talk about something else. Like lets hear some big freaking initiation details! How'd it go?" Z asks. "Are you feeling more womanly? Or more witchy?"

"Well, Sascha would probably say I'm feeling more *bitchy* than usual, but . . ." Margo pauses, as all of our eyes go wide.

I think we're all amazed Margo is a little more self-aware than we might have given her credit for.

"But," she continues, "let's just say you all need to throw away any assumptions you have about what it is we do, and go to your initiation prepared to have the rug pulled out from under your feet."

"Why? What did they tell you?" Dani whispers, her eyes bugging out.

"Yeah," Z says. "You can't leave us hanging."

Margo doesn't say anything and I can almost hear her mind working out whether Helena's pet hunter can buck the rules and spill initiation secrets. I think she wants to tell us— she wouldn't have laid the whole *rug* thing on us if she wasn't at least thinking about it.

"Margo, you can tell us," I say. "We won't let on, right?"

Dani and Z nod.

"I can't," she says finally. She turns and picks her broom off the ground and wipes the dirt off the handle. "We just can't be screwing around with hunts, okay?"

A car pulls up near the dugout and we all freeze.

"Is that Troy and Andrew?" I ask. "We'd better cloak!"

"No," Zahara says. "My mom said Michael was going to 'divert them' from keeping their *date* with Kelsey."

"Look, it's the van," Dani says. "It's probably Michael or maybe Connor." She wrinkles her brow. "But we don't need a cleanup tonight 'cause it was a . . ."

Margo puts her hands on her hips and glares at Dani.

"Well, you know," Dani says, shrugging her shoulders.

My heart races, hoping I'll get to see Connor again. The van lights go off, but it's Michael who opens the door and gets out.

We head over, and Michael puts an arm around Dani and Zahara's shoulders. "I was on decoy duty, so my mom told me what was going down tonight. I was kind of friends with Kelsey, and I know Sascha was, too." Michael looks around at us. "Where is Sascha—did she leave already?"

"Yeah, she took it kind of hard," I say, glaring at Margo.

Michael nods, like he's not surprised. "Well, I didn't know how you all would be doing, and even though it's against the rules, I thought you might like a ride home in a warm van instead of having to stick it in the cold tonight."

Margo and Zahara look at each other. Z gives the slightest shake of her head, and I know she's following Margo's lead and pulling herself back into traditional icy-hunter mode. I can't help but wonder if she'd be able to do it so quickly if Kelsey's body was still lying on the ground by the dugout.

"Thanks," Margo says, "but I think we should fly home. Kelsey won't be the last person we know on the hunt list, and we need to keep with the program. Right, *everyone?*"

"Yeah, right," Zahara says, slipping out from under Michael's arm. She takes out the flask from her cloak and takes a long swig, and then hands it over to Margo.

"Hunt list?" I ask.

Margo chokes on the brandy.

"Oh, my God!" I say. "Is that how it works—is there a *list* of spooks we go after?"

"What?" Margo sputters. "No! Well, sort of, but . . ."

"Come on, Margo!" I say. "We're all going to find out what's going on in a few weeks anyway—so what's the big deal? Just tell us how a spook gets on the list. How did Kelsey end up being tonight's hunt?"

"Look!" Margo says. "It's complicated—and Helena would kill me if I said anything." Margo suddenly looks worried. "Don't tell her I said anything, okay? And if she asks about tonight, make sure you tell her it was *me* who finished Kelsey off." She pauses and looks at us one at a time with a steely face. "And I won't tell her how I found you all standing around not doing your job."

Margo hands me the flask and mounts her broom. "There is one thing I can tell you, Jules." She reaches into her cloak and pulls out the star necklace—the inside of the stone flashes and glimmers with light. "Not showing your loyalty can get you or your family in a *hell* of a lot of trouble." She tips her head toward Michael. "I suggest you keep your mouth shut, too! You coming, Z?"

"Yeah! Um, I'll see you guys tomorrow," she says slowly. She gets on her stick and looks back at me. She shrugs and then they both take off in a shimmer as their cloaking spell takes effect.

They vanish into the low clouds, and Michael clears his throat. "Wow. I thought this was going to be a tough one tonight—but I didn't think it would be this bad."

I take a Sascha-sized gulp of brandy and shudder as it burns its way down my throat. "You know what I think? I think I'll take that ride, Michael."

7

"So how do you think someone gets on the list?"
I ask. I clutch the armrest as Michael takes a corner too fast.

"We're not sure if there really is a list," Dani says from the
backseat.

"Are you kidding? Did you see how scared Margo was
when that slipped out? There's a list! Michael, what do they
tell you when you're on cleanup crew?"

"Just that they've tracked someone down, and then they
give us the address where they are. Sometimes they tell Connor
and me personal info, like that last guy—the wolf—my mom
told us he might be interested in joining me out in the woods
behind the bar, if you know what I mean."

"But how could they know that?" I ask.

"Crystal ball?" Michael says.

Dani leans forward and nods. "Mrs. Keyes has one, she could be using it to track people down, or maybe she uses a spell to locate them."

"But what about Kelsey? She was supposed to meet Troy and Andrew, so how did they know to send you over there to make sure they didn't show up and witness the kill? If she was using a crystal ball, she'd have to be watching Kelsey 24/7 to happen upon that information."

"I don't know. They just told me to have a couple of cases of cold beer in the back of the van, park it by Troy's house, and loosen a battery cable. I was supposed to convince them partying would be better than being bitten. Not that I mentioned Kelsey or anything, but being underage and unemployed, they were more than happy to accept some free booze in return for tightening up the cable for me. Actually, Andrew seemed pretty relieved they were going to take the beer back to Troy's. But you know what? Troy's been bitten before—I could see marks on him."

"Oh!" Dani says. "That means Kelsey's probably, you know, snacked on him before."

I nod. "And it also means vamps don't always turn their prey—something we were told they do."

Dani and I exchange looks, and I know we're both wondering if what she'd read on that message board is true.

"And Kelsey could've been telling the truth when she

said she wasn't going to reveal to us," Dani says.

"And maybe we didn't have to dust her," I add.

Dani shakes her head. "What matters is she wasn't human anymore. Maybe she wasn't going to go after *us*, but she was fully capable of it."

"Yeah, and Z did say she'd already turned some other people, but still, I don't think this whole gig is quite what we thought it was. If there's a list, it means someone—maybe Helena—is making some sort of decision about who we go after and when we do it," I say.

"Geez, Jules," Dani says, swatting me on the shoulder. "You're making it sound like there's some evil plot. I just figured Helena makes a list of baddies as the coven hears about them, and then someone does research to make our job a little easier."

My shoulders slump. "Yeah, I guess." I watch the houses go by as we near my neighborhood. What Dani said makes sense, I think, but it doesn't explain why Margo was all freaked out—and she *was* freaked out. "Why all the secrecy, then? Why not tell us exactly what's going on instead of waiting for the stupid birthday initiation crap?"

Michael laughs. "Because you witches are *totally* anal about tradition! Margo and Z wouldn't even get in the van because you're supposed to fly home after a kill. Hell, you're probably breaking all sorts of covenants riding home with me."

"I know, it's so stupid—what does it *matter* if we stick it or get a ride home?" I ask. "And why these capes? Loved getting shit about them from Kelsey tonight. She asked about our lame 'Little Red Riding Hood' look."

Michael laughs as he slows the van to a stop in front of my house. "Yeah, the capes are a little retro."

"Hey, keep going," Dani says. "I saw the kitchen lights on—maybe you should let us out down the street, I'll fly home and it will look like you did, too. I don't want any of us to get in trouble."

He accelerates and pulls over farther down the block by the woods.

"Viva la revolution!" I say.

"I'm just feeling a little spooked, all right? I mean all this talk about lists and traditions, well—remember the time Mrs. Keyes reamed me out because I hadn't made the binders tight enough and they fell apart before they hit the ground?"

"She was mad the vamp got away," I say. "This is just a ride."

"Well, you never know what's gonna make her go nuts," Dani says. "She came down on Z that time for showing up on a hunt without a stake even though we were going after a wolf!"

"Okay, fine," I say, opening the door. "But I plan on asking my mom a few things when I get in. Thanks for the ride,

Michael. It was really nice not having to fly home in the cold *even* if we get in trouble!"

Dani gets out and shakes her head. "I can't help it if Mrs. Keyes scares the crap out of me!"

"Mrs. Keyes scares the crap out of everyone!" Michael says. "But I'll keep this illicit ride home under wraps. If you guys don't have another hunt tomorrow, I'll see you in school."

Michael drives off, and Dani turns to me.

"Are you really going to ask your mom about the list?" she asks, mounting her broom. "Margo said not to."

"Damn straight I am. Just because you're too chicken to buck tradition, doesn't mean I am."

"Too chicken to buck tradition? Oh, please. I rode in the van same as you. I just like to keep my rebellion under the radar. Let me know if your mom says anything interesting."

"Will do."

Dani says the cloaking spell and takes off. I walk toward my house. As I pass the side garden, I'm tempted to sneak out to Mom's workshop to make sure Connor cleaned up, but I want to catch her before she heads to bed.

I open the kitchen door and smell mint hot chocolate. I walk in and see two mugs out on the counter and a pot steaming on the stovetop next to the cauldron.

"I'm home!"

Mom comes in tying her blue bathrobe sash tight. "I got home just a bit ago and thought I'd wait up in case you wanted to talk. I know that girl went to school with you all. Did you know her well?"

"We had a couple of classes together and we worked on a group project once, but Sascha was the only one that was kind of friends with her." I decide to not mention Michael. I throw my cape over a chair, and spot the Ouroboros ring. Does my mom know about it? I get up and turn the burner off, and then I pull my sweater sleeves over my hands so just my fingertips are showing. "Brrrr, I'm still cold. This will warm me up, though." I fill up the mugs and bring them over to the table, wondering how long I can hide the stupid ring. "It was a tough kill, though."

Mom blows across the top of the milk. "Did she attack before you bound her?"

"No! That's what made it so hard. She just wanted to hang out with us."

"Well," Mom says with a little laugh, "that's not likely, but who ended up staking her?"

I take a sip and burn my tongue. "Ow! Margo did it. She showed up late, but once she saw Kelsey bound by home plate, she staked her without blinking an eye."

The corners of Mom's lips curl up and I wonder why this news makes her smile.

"So now that Kelsey's taken care of, who's next on *the list*? Anyone I know?"

Mom's smile dissolves in a flash. "What are you talking about?"

"It's okay, Mom. Margo let it slip out that there's a list of creatures we have to hunt. It's not like it's a big deal."

She smiles again, but I can tell it's forced. She takes a sip of chocolate, obviously weighing her response carefully. "What else did Margo say?"

"Nothing much, but I figured since I knew, we didn't have to wait until my birthday for you to tell me the ins and outs of who gets knocked off the secret list next."

She takes another sip and nods her head. "Well," she says slowly, "there is a list—I'm not sure I would use the word *secret*, though."

I stifle my desire to yell *I knew it* and keep my poker face going. "It was a secret to me, but how does someone get on the not so secret list?"

"We simply note the names of creatures we find out are in the area. When we get more information and pin down a location, we send you girls after them. The end."

"But how do you get the information?" I ask, thinking she's purposefully trying to sound very casual about this.

"Let's save some surprises for your initiation, shall we?"

She gets up from the table and pours the rest of her hot chocolate into the sink.

"How did Kelsey get to be tonight's hunt?" I ask, not letting it go. "How did you know to send Michael after Troy and Andrew?"

"Word gets around," she says stiffly.

I raise my eyebrows. "What, do we have an 800 number so people can call in with anonymous tips?" I pretend to flip open my cell phone. "Hello, I overheard some people planning a vampire orgy—you should show up at the baseball dugout at eleven o'clock."

Mom looks at me with raised eyebrows. "I'm a bit surprised you're being so cavalier about this after tonight's hunt."

"And I think you're trying to change the subject."

Mom stares at me, and then shakes her head with an exasperated huff. "Honey, it's been a long day."

"You always say that when you don't want to talk!"

"It was a long day! The initiation was draining, and I have a lot of work to do in the shop tomorrow. Let's call it a night. We can talk more after I get these new witch balls done." She gives me that forced smile again, and starts to walk toward the stairs.

I get up and stand in front of her, blocking the way. "Did you know vamps don't turn everyone they bite? Kelsey bit Troy but she didn't turn him. And she didn't attack us—she didn't even show her fangs until we tried to bind her."

Mom squeezes her eyes shut for a few seconds and sighs. "Yes, occasionally a vampire won't turn someone, and maybe Kelsey was feeling the loss of her old life and wanted to reconnect by talking with you. But at the end of the day—or night, I should say—vampires are soulless monsters capable of murder. And just because Kelsey hadn't turned that young man, doesn't mean she wasn't going to. You don't know what twisted game she was playing with him."

"But you told us they *always* turn their victims. . . ."

"Into new vampires. Yes. I suppose we didn't feel it necessary to point out that there are always exceptions, but I thought at seventeen years of age you might have figured that out!"

Mom glares at me with wide eyes, and I start feeling really stupid. Of course, they'd be keeping a list—how else would they keep track of sightings? And can I really say Kelsey wouldn't have attacked us?

No.

But why was Margo so upset, then? Was she just being her usual anal self?

"I'm sorry," I say, and step aside. "I don't know why I got it in my head there was some deep, dark conspiracy. But if you'd just tell us everything up front, my mind wouldn't go wild trying to fill in the blanks."

Mom reaches out and squeezes my hand, but her face looks pinched and worried, and not at all like she's happy she's won this argument. "Maybe it is time to look into how we're doing things—the world is changing so very rapidly and perhaps we finally need to address the fact you girls are not at all like the past generations of hunters.

"I'll talk to the inner circle—Margo included—and see if we can start a dialogue about looking toward a more modern future. Knowing you girls, I can't imagine your children will be any easier to deal with! I can't promise any rapid reforms, but I'll see what I can do."

"Thanks, Mom," I say hugging her—hardly believing I've finally convinced her to talk to Helena and everyone else. "I'll clean up the dishes."

"Okay, and then off to bed."

I bring my cup to the sink and fill the pot with warm soapy water. I pour some of the dish soap on my hand and soap up my ring finger. I try to pull off the Ouroboros, but it hisses at me and gulps down its tail until I feel like it's going to cut off the circulation in my finger. "Fine!" I hiss back at it quietly. I rinse the soap off, and the snake relaxes its grip and returns to its hard metallic state.

In my room, I see Connor's put the white pumpkin with the heart carved in it on my bedside table. I point my palm toward the candle. "Light," I whisper, thinking that's exactly how I feel—light and happy. The pumpkin glows and I love that Connor left it here.

And I love that Connor and I will be out in the open soon, that I'll be able to skip the broom rides in the winter, and maybe we can even burn the stupid capes in a bonfire!

I pull my sweater off and throw it to the floor on top of my jeans. I sigh and pick them up and put them in the laundry basket. I grab all the other clothes and throw them in, too. This will show Mom I'm maturing into a responsible witch, I think.

I take my nightshirt off the bed and pull it on—but it snags on one of the points of my star necklace. I reach up and grab the turquoise center and pull the tip out of the fabric. The Ouroboros hisses, opens its mouth, and falls off my finger. I jump back as it twists and wiggles near my feet—snapping at the air with its tiny fanged mouth. It finally finds its tail, takes two quick swallows, and reforms into a solid circle.

I stare at the ring. After a few seconds I nudge it with my foot, and when it doesn't move, I grab a pen off my desk and lift it up. I clear a spot in my junk drawer in my dresser, drop it in, and catch a glimpse of my necklace in the mirror. The stone is glowing, and I smile, knowing the necklace overpowered the ring. I pick up the card that came with the necklace. Turquoise, December's birthstone, protects the wearer

FROM EVIL, AND WARNS OF APPROACHING DANGER.

I shut the drawer slowly and the stone dims. Well, I think that ring more than qualifies as evil—even if what it does is good. The necklace would probably react like that around anything that came straight from hell.

I get in bed and pull the covers up to my chin. As my heart slows and the adrenaline stops pumping, I think this night hasn't ended so badly. The ring is off, Mom will talk to Helena—things are going to get better.

My finger throbs from where the Ouroboros was. I gently rub it, wondering if Connor got all the details about it right. There's got to be more info about the ring somewhere, especially if Helena wanted it so badly. I can hardly believe she'd have us hack off a demon's finger for a ring that just lets the wearer know the giver is telling the truth. One thing is for sure—I'm giving it back to Connor and then he can put it back in his mom's little treasure room where I'll never have to see it again!

I throw a spell to blow the candle out. I wonder what other goodies Helena has in there? Tomorrow I'll ask Connor to show me.

8

"Well, at least you know you were right about the ring moving that night," I say to Dani the next day.

"I still can't believe he gave it to you," Dani says, sitting at my desk, poking the Ouroboros with a pen.

"Nothing says love like a ring hacked off a demon!"

Dani shudders. "I can still hear its blood sizzling in my head."

"At least the pumpkins were sweet," I say, trying to defend Connor's honor. I reach over and light the candle again with my hand, and then lean back on my pillows. "Plus, he was more concerned about me trusting him than where the ring came from."

She pulls the ring around in a circle across the desktop with the pen and shakes her head. "Yeah, after what he pulled,

I guess he knew he needed something more than a couple of squashes." She turns and looks at me with raised eyebrows. "I still don't see why you couldn't go over to his house today— I mean with his mom coming over to work with your mom, the timing would be perfect."

"But we don't know how long she'll be here, and since his mom is going to be out of town for a few days next week after Sascha's initiation—I have an open invitation to visit then."

"Oh?" Dani gives me a "what are you planning" look. "Are you going to take him up on it?"

"Damned straight I am!" I pull my knees up and lean my chin on them. "At least we won't have to sneak around much longer."

"Jules," Dani says, brow furrowed. "Just because your mom said she'd talk to Mrs. Keyes . . ."

"And don't forget Margo!"

"Uh, are *you* forgetting Margo is just as obsessed with the stupid traditions as Mrs. Keyes is?"

I give her a look.

"Okay, no one comes close to Helena, but like I was *trying* to say, just because your mom suggests some people talk about change, doesn't mean it's gonna happen."

"But after our birthdays we'll all be in the inner circle and we can force the issue! You know—out with the old, in with the new stuff."

Dani purses her lips. "Maybe, but I don't think you should go out and burn your cape just yet." She hooks the ring on the pen, holds it up to her face, and then turns to me—her eyes wide. "Put it on so I can see it move—it was so dark that night we got it I didn't get a good look!"

"Yeah, no freaking way! Look at my finger, it's still all red."

"Oh, come on, just for a second. You can use the necklace to get it off again."

"We don't know how much charge is left in the necklace, but if you want to see it move so badly, you can put it on. It's really cute when it hisses and cuts the circulation off."

"Never mind." Dani puts the ring down and pushes the chair back and walks over to my bed. "So what kind of stuff do you think Mrs. Keyes has stored away in her secret room? Do you think we'll get to see it after our initiations? Oh! Maybe the initiation takes *place* in the secret room—that would be cool."

"Gee," I say. "A room full of leftover nightmare crap— sounds great. Maybe that vest we got off that wolf freshman year will be in it. Maybe if you ask really nicely, Helena will let you wear it."

"Ew!" Dani wrinkles her nose. "The one with all the eye- balls sewn on it, do you think she has it? I just figured they'd burn it or something."

"I'll have to ask Connor, but that was definitely *the* most fucked-up article of clothing I've ever seen!" I shudder, picturing the eyes rolling around and blinking. And they were all shades of blues, and I remember thinking how glad I was mine are brown!

Dani's phone starts playing "Genie in a Bottle," and I laugh. "Nice ringtone! If you were wearing the vest all the eyes would be rolling toward the ceiling."

She sticks her tongue out at me and then reaches over to her purse. She fishes her phone out and gasps. "Oh, my God! It's him—it's Evan!" Dani waves the phone frantically in my face. "What do I do?"

"Answer it!"

"Right!" She pushes the button and takes a quick breath. "Hi, Evan . . . I'm just hanging out with Jules at her house. . . . Yeah, I could definitely use some help!"

Dani's eyes glitter and she mouths the words *library* and *study* to me.

"Finn, too? Oh, sure that's fine." Dani curls her lip up in a mock snarl. "I just need to get my stuff at my house and I'll be right over. . . . Jules? Um, I'll have to ask her, but maybe. . . . Okay, I'll see you soon."

She pushes the END button and stamps her feet up and down. "I have a date!" she squeals.

"Shh! My mom is downstairs, and Mrs. Keyes could already be here!"

"I have a date," she whispers. "And my heart is pounding a mile a minute, and I'm profusely sweating, and I think I need to put on some more deodorant."

I laugh. "What did he say?"

"He's going to the library to study for the next chem quiz and wanted to know if I wanted to meet him there." She looks at me with wide eyes. "This is a date, right? Or did he just want to study and I'm totally making a fool of myself right now?"

"I . . ."

"If it really was a date," she interrupts, "he wouldn't have asked you to come along—you're not even taking chem!"

"It's a date. And he was probably just being polite when he invited me because you're at my house. But Finn is in your class, right? So that means Evan already has someone to study with, which means he doesn't need you to come, he *wants* you to."

"He *wants* me," Dani says, and bites her lip. She shakes her fist in the air and then jumps up off my bed. "We have to get going—and you're coming!"

She tries to pull me up off the bed, but I yank my hand out of hers. "Don't you want to be alone with him?"

"Yes, that's why you're coming—you have to get rid of Finn."

"How am I going to do that?"

"I don't care how you do it—cast a spell or something. Just make sure Evan and I have some alone time." She pauses. "No, maybe it's better it's a group study date—but you still have to come because I might faint."

"Fine, I'll come, and if you think you're ready for some *alone time*, just give me a signal and I'll figure out some way to get rid of Finn. I'll drive—my mom is supposed to be working all day so it should be fine."

Dani grabs my hand again and I let her pull me up this time. "Great, let's go!" she says. "Wait! You shouldn't leave that burning." She points to the pumpkin. "*Out!*"

I shake my head and then we're both laughing as we race down the stairs. We stop midway. Mrs. Keyes is standing in the kitchen, looking up at us. Her white hair is pulled back in a tight braid making her look more severe than usual.

"Ladies," she says coldly. "Something funny?"

Dani and I look at each other, and I see the color drain from her cheeks. We walk slowly the rest of the way down and I really do wonder if Dani will up and faint.

"Hi, Mrs. Keyes," I say.

Mrs. Keyes's eyes bore into me and I just know she's thinking about Connor and me—or maybe Mom told her about all the stuff I want to change. I keep a happy smile plastered on despite the fact my cheeks are burning and my legs feel weak.

"Hi," Dani mumbles.

"We're just going to head off to the library. Dani's got a big chem thing to study for and I have some books I need to check out for a paper."

I resist the urge to brush my bangs aside and keep smiling, hoping Mrs. Keyes can't tell I'm lying.

She tilts her head and looks quizzically at us. "Studying? On such a lovely day?"

Her voices oozes with fake sincerity, and I wonder how it's possible that someone like her could be Connor's mother. We stand there silently and I realize Dani is too scared to help me out.

"Yeah, we try to get stuff done in the day in case we have to go on a hunt in the evenings."

Dani lets out a nervous laugh. "Yeah," she says, looking back and forth between Mrs. Keyes and me with a crazed look in her eyes. "It's been absolutely nutso lately, but you, um, you know that because you're in charge and all. Ha."

I have to get Dani out of here fast before she blows this. Luckily, Mom comes in wearing an old pair of overalls.

"Hi, girls. We were just heading out to the shop. Helena is going to help me with the new balls."

Mrs. Keyes's snaky smile widens—I half expect a forked tongue to come zipping out and smell the fear coming off us. "The girls were just heading off to spend this lovely day in the li-brar-y," she says slowly.

"Great," Mom says. "I hope this means your grades will be a little better this time."

"Oh, I always get straight A's," Dani says.

I swat Dani on the shoulder.

Dani grimaces at me. "Oh, she meant—well, it's not like you flunked anything."

"It's just math I have trouble with, I get A's and B's in everything else!"

Mom puts her hands on her hips.

"Okay, I get an occasional C in some of my other classes," I say, embarrassed Mrs. Keyes probably thinks I'm some idiot not worthy of her son. Not that she thinks I'm worthy anyway. I grab my purse that is hanging on one of the kitchen chairs and take the keys off the counter. "Let's just go—I can use the car, right?"

"Sure, sweetie."

Dani and I walk outside, and we both exhale when we get in the car.

"You know, I think I'd rather go another round with the Ouroboros ring than deal with Mrs. Keyes," I say. "Did you hear the way she was all drippy sweet 'on such a lovely day'?"

"Yeah," Dani says. "Like she thought we were lying or something."

"We were lying."

"No, not really. I'm going to the library to study! I can't help it if Evan will just happen to be there."

"You're right. Let's get your stuff and get you ready for your date!"

"Are you sure I look okay?" Dani asks for the millionth time as we open the library door.

"Yes!"

"Maybe I shouldn't have curled my hair—maybe I should've left it straight. It's usually straight at school and so maybe he won't recognize me or maybe he hates curly hair."

I look at the soft brown curls framing Dani's face and smile. "You look beautiful."

She smiles for a second and then looks down at her pants. "But do these make me look fat? Maybe I should've worn a skirt. I still can't believe there isn't a spell to get rid of cellulite—and believe me, I've looked for one!"

"Dani, he likes you—period. Relax."

We walk past the circulation desk, and Dani points to a table near the biography section. "There he is—alone!" She turns to me with determined eyes. "Make yourself scarce!"

I laugh as she rushes over to Evan. I wave to him from where I am, glad Dani's ready to tackle this date without my help. I glance around for Finn, but maybe Evan's given him his marching orders, too. I watch Dani sit down right next to him instead of across the table and give her a silent *you go, girl*. Evan smiles shyly at her, and immediately opens his textbook, but he also moves his chair closer to her so I know there's hope.

Since I didn't bring any actual work to do—cue Mom's disapproving *tsk*—I decide to head to the newly remodeled Teen Room. I walk up the ramp to the old part of the library where they stuck it, so the teenagers wouldn't bother the other patrons in the new addition. I squint when I walk under the FRESH BOOKS sign hanging above the entryway, and wonder which librarian thought teens would dig fluorescent green paint on the walls.

Then I wonder if Miss Melissa were still alive if she would've suggested a better color.

At least they have some couches. I roll my eyes as I walk past a popular vamp book sitting on an end cap. I tried to read it once, but couldn't get past the whole romantic, misunderstood vamp shtick. And there's just something totally creepy about a thousand-year-old vamp seducing a high school freshman—talk about extreme jailbait.

I was half tempted to write to the author, but I knew he'd just think I was a nut job for suggesting there was nothing romantic about *real* vampires. Of course, Dani's read it and its sequels at least six times, and she keeps insisting I give the book another try.

I skim the shelves and pick something a little more teen angsty. After hunting for over four years, normal teen drama is more my kind of escapist literature. I sink in the couch—glad the "lovely day" has guaranteed most kids are outside doing something and I can be alone.

"I know what you are."

I jump as Finn sits down on the overstuffed chair opposite me. His face is expressionless—his green eyes locked on to mine.

"I'm reading?" I say, holding up my book, not sure what he meant. I want to look away, but for some reason I feel like I shouldn't. Like this is some sort of turf thing.

He runs his fingers through his shaggy black hair, and curls his lip up like I'm a piece of dirt. "I know what you are, and if you or Dani do anything to hurt Evan you'll have to deal with me."

"Hurt Evan? What are you talking about?" I put my hands up and shrug my shoulders. "They're studying. Are you worried they may overtax a few synapses?"

Finn sniffs the air and seems to relax a bit. He scans the room and then looks back at me. "I know you're a witch."

I take in a ragged breath as a chill passes over me. I think of all the times I've run into Finn while I was cloaked and thought he saw me. The way he stares at Sascha. How does he know?

He leans in toward me and sniffs again. I decide he's got some sort of extrasensory thing going and my mind races trying to figure out what I can say to convince him he's wrong.

"The question is—are you a good witch or a bad witch?"

"Good!" I blurt out before I can stop myself.

Finn laughs, and I just sit there staring at him open-mouthed, wondering what the hell just happened.

"Yeah, that's what I figured," he says. He puts his black boots up on the coffee table separating us and pulls at the knees of his faded jeans. "Evan thought so, too, but I wanted to be sure. He's not exactly the most socially adept guy. I didn't want you *witches* messing with him."

"How did you know? How did Evan know?" As soon as the words leave my mouth I could kick myself. I should have denied the whole thing—called him crazy—protected our secret.

"Let's just say I can smell a witch a mile away, but I had to be sure you weren't the kind of witch who goes around sacrificing puppies under a new moon so you can put your mojo on some poor guy."

Now I get mad. "You actually think Dani or I would sacrifice puppies?"

Finn puts his feet down and leans in toward me. "Relax. Margo is the only one I could picture doing that."

"Margo may be a bitch but she wouldn't . . ."

"God, you're easy to bait! This whole thing took a lot less time than I thought it would. I expected you to at least deny it for a while."

I cover my eyes with my hands and shake my head. I am in such deep shit. The coven has only had to move two times since it was formed, and the last thing I want is to be the cause of the next mass exodus.

"Okay, so you know, what now?" I cock my head and look him up and down, trying very hard to channel Helena. "Do I erase your memory? Turn you into a toad? Make a voodoo doll and walk you into the path of an oncoming truck?"

Finn laughs and I'm guessing I wasn't too convincing.

"I'll take option two, but only if you make it a frog— they're much cooler than toads."

"Laugh all you want, but there are some witches I know who wouldn't hesitate going after you if they thought you might talk."

"Don't worry. I'm not going to rat you out—and really, who would believe me if I did? My only purpose here today was to make sure my man, Evan, was going to come out of his first foray into romance unscathed."

I look at him smiling and all relaxed in his chair. We've studied body language to help us know when it's the right time to throw binders, and everything tells me Finn is being sincere. "Okay, but you have to tell me how you know about us."

"If I told you it would take away my air of mystery that you witches all dig."

"Oh, please."

"I'm just shitting you," Finn says. He smiles even wider and takes a pack of gum out of the front pocket of his flannel shirt. He pops a piece in his mouth and then throws one across the table to me. "Maybe if I get to know you better, I'll let you in on my little secret. But right now I'm gonna give Evan the signal that Dani's safe to pillage."

"What!"

"Sorry—guy talk. Safe to *date*. But I think we can both agree it's safe to leave them alone now. I have to change the oil in my grandmother's car, and you can go home and, uh—boil fairies. Okay?"

I scoff and shake my head. "You do know that boiling even the smallest of pixies would bring the wrath of the fairy court down on you so fast you'd be wishing I *had* turned you into a toad, right?"

"Well, I guess I better go out and empty that jelly jar I filled last night, before Tinker Bell and her friends start kicking my butt, eh?"

I laugh. "I'd say that would be a good idea."

"Thanks for the tip!" He gets up and takes his car keys out of his pocket.

"Wait, how do I know *Evan* is safe for Dani to date?

Maybe I should be warning her to stay away from him!"

Finn tilts his head down and gives me an "are you totally without clues" look. "The guy would wear pocket protectors if he didn't think he'd get beat up for it. He's got the wild-haired Einstein poster hanging above his headboard, and he's never looked at porn.

"And no, before you ask, he's not gay. He's just the by-product of overprotective, mega-nerd parents. I'd tell Dani if she wants some action she should make the first, and possibly second and third moves." He winks and heads toward the ramp into the main library. "See you around, witchy-poo!"

I watch him swagger down, his boots clomping, and know I should tell my mom about this. But there'd be too many questions I don't want to answer. That Dani wouldn't want to answer, too. And who knows, maybe Helena *would* do something to Evan and Finn. My stomach rolls nervously.

Or me.

What would she do if she found out I'd just been chatting about fairies with a mere mortal?

I chew on my thumbnail and think maybe she'd decide that the idiot who didn't deny being a witch could *never* be with Connor no matter what changes the coven makes.

I pick up the book lying next to me and gently tap it on my forehead. "I-am-such-an-idiot," I whisper between thwonks.

As long as Finn keeps it quiet I should be okay. I think.

I get up and walk toward the stacks. Just concentrate on things changing—and Connor's house next week, I tell myself.

Just the thought of us alone—in his room with no chance of interruption—makes me feel warm all over. A happy shiver runs down my spine as I put the book back on the shelf. I lick my lips and wish Connor were with me right now.

I head out to the main part of the library and catch Dani's eye. She beams at me. I point toward the door and wave. She nods and I wonder how she's going to take the news that her would-be boyfriend knows she's a witch.

I smile. Maybe her fantasy wasn't too far off.

9

"My mom bought this great long underwear for flying. It's really warm, but it's not the ultra-thick bulky kind," Dani yells.

Dani keeps talking, but the wind is whipping around so much it's hard to hear her, and really all I can think about is Sascha filling us in on the supersecret ceremony tonight after her initiation is over.

"Are you listening?" Dani calls out.

"*What*?" I say.

"I said, at first I was mad—like she thought the bulky stuff would just make me look fatter, but then I figured I was being paranoid and she probably thought I'd just like some newer stuff, you know?"

I'm about to tell Dani to just concentrate on not getting

knocked off her broom instead of rambling on about long underwear, but we're already heading lower toward the meeting spot and the wind is easing up.

I tilt my broom down, careful to clear the tall pines surrounding the opening in the woods.

"Shit!" Dani yells.

I look back and see her foot tangled briefly in a treetop. She tugs it out and her broom lurches forward. I stifle a laugh as she lands ahead of me missing a shoe.

"Crap! Mud! My foot is soaked." She points her hand toward the base of the trees we just cleared. "*Return!*"

"Geez," she says when the shoe doesn't return. She points up higher in the trees. "*Return!*" she says louder.

I hear branches breaking, and then a clog comes flying toward us, just missing my head before hitting the ground behind us.

"You're wearing clogs on a broomstick?" I ask incredulously. I pick it up, careful to avoid the mud covering it, and hand it to her.

"Sorry, I wasn't exactly thinking straight at one o'clock in the morning. My mother was at me to get going so I just grabbed these."

She slips it on her foot and we walk over to some benches surrounding a stone fire-pit, a short distance from a lean-to. Empty beer bottles litter the ground, and I'm guessing the last people here were partying rather than camping.

"We're the first ones," I say, scanning the sky for anyone else.

"I hope they get here soon—it feels like winter already," Dani says. "What do you think it'll be tonight, vamp or wolf? I hope it's not a demon. What with that ring Connor gave you and that stupid vest you reminded me of, I don't feel like dealing with them tonight."

"How about a ghost? We haven't done one of those in ages."

Dani looks around the campsite and shakes her head. "I doubt there's any ghosts here, but we don't usually have to hunt them because they don't typically kill people. We just go after them when . . ."

"Dani."

"I'm doing it again, aren't I?"

I nod. "Yeah. I know why we don't usually go after ghosts."

"Well, I thought we'd have a hunt tonight. Look." Dani pulls her necklace out and holds up the star, its center swirling with light. "It started just before I got to the coven house for Sascha's initiation. But then we went home, and my mom came home, so I thought I could actually get a decent night's sleep before my quiz tomorrow." Dani rubs her hands together, and then pulls them under her cape. "I'm beginning to think our birthdays are bringing us bad luck," Dani adds.

"Maybe it's your chem quizzes. But my necklace didn't do anything tonight—maybe it needs a recharge. Did you notice Margo hasn't been wearing hers? I guess we are oh-for-three on her birthday presents."

"Yeah," Dani says. "I can't believe she couldn't at least pretend to like the lavender stuff. I mean, it's totally rude to tell people the stuff they gave you smells like crappy, old-lady perfume."

"Ha!" I say. "Maybe she figured out we only got it for her because she's such a bitch, and lavender is supposed to calm you down."

"Maybe she likes being a bitch."

"Look, here comes someone," I say, pointing up. As the figure comes closer, I see it's Z.

Suddenly Margo comes streaking past her and lands on her feet running. "I win!"

Zahara lands and walks toward us. "I wasn't *racing* you, Margo," she says, sounding pissed.

I can hear her stud clicking against her teeth in a steady rhythm.

Margo smiles. "I still win." She blows out a thin line of breath that freezes and then breaks up over her head. "No birthday girl yet?"

"I'm here," Sascha says behind us and we all jump.

"God," Dani says. "Have you been here the whole time?"

Sascha walks out into the clearing, taking a long swig from the flask. "Wolf tonight," she says. "Gotta be quick about it," she says in a singsong voice. "She's supposed to meet here for a payoff." She takes another long drink. "Oops," she says, giggling. "I don't think I was supposed to tell you uninitiated people that!" She throws an arm around Margo and hiccups. "But you can know!"

Margo pushes her away and Sascha falls to the ground.

"Hey!" she giggles. "That wasn't nice. Are you afraid someone's going to get—"

"Shut the hell up!" Margo yells. "Are you insane?"

Dani, Z, and I exchange looks. Frosty breath puffs out from our open mouths.

"Are you okay?" I ask as I help Sascha up.

"I'm fine," she says, brushing mud and leaves off her hands. "Just a happy hunter."

"Will someone tell us what's going on?" Z says. "All this cryptic shit is totally getting on my nerves."

Sascha laughs. "Isn't it annoying? But guess what? Our mothers weren't just being tools about all the *cryptic shit*— there really *is* a good reason why they wait until our birthdays to dump a shitload of shit on us."

She raises the flask to her lips again, and Margo snatches it away. "Just shut up, okay? Just shut up and I won't tell anyone what you just did."

"Did they tell *you* what happened to my dad, Margo?" Sascha whispers.

"Just stop," Margo pleads.

"Why? My big mouth doesn't affect you!"

"It might! You don't know."

"Guys!" I interrupt. "Cut the crap and tell us what's going on."

Sascha tilts her head at Margo and sways a bit. "We can word it carefully. You don't honestly believe we can't—"

"Look," Dani says, "someone's coming."

Headlights work their way up through the trees along the dirt road.

"Shit," I say. "She's here—what are we doing?"

"Wonder drunk is supposed to have all the details," Margo hisses as we slowly retreat toward the forest's edge.

Sascha giggles again, and Z grabs her cape. "Get it together and tell us what the deal with the wolf is," she says through clenched teeth. "Is it just one?"

Sascha pushes Z off her. "Yeah. It's just one lone wolf, and she's expecting to meet someone for a payoff. We get her, and then Connor cleans up."

My heart skips a beat.

"What about Michael—won't he be here, too?" Dani asks.

"Tonight it's just Connor." Sascha points toward a lean-to just off the dirt road. "He's already over there waiting."

I see the van parked. As the other car—some sort of sports coupe—pulls up toward it, Connor flashes his lights a few times. Connor is the person she's meeting?

"Is there anything else we need to know?" Margo asks.

Sascha heads over to the car. "Nope—just some little detail I need to take care of—I'm sure they're testing me." She looks back and gives Margo a big, cheesy smile. "And don't worry, Margo, I'll make the inner circle proud."

Margo rushes up to Sascha. I strain to hear what she's saying, but the wind roars past carrying her words away.

Sascha pulls out her star necklace, and wraps her hand around it. Her whole body goes rigid for a second and then she breaks into a run.

"*What is going on?*" Dani whispers to me as we hurry after her.

"I don't know."

Connor gets out of the van and holds up a white envelope. "All set for you, Diane."

A tall woman with long, white hair opens the car door. "Great," she says. "And you tell your mom it's been a pleasure doing . . ."

"*Silence!*" Sascha screams, running at her. A bolt of white light streaks from her palm and hits the woman in the head knocking her down. "We bind you to the earth!" Sascha throws a binder, and the mud and debris on the ground coil up and pin her down on her back.

"Nice work," Connor says.

I hope he didn't mean that.

I purposefully avoid making eye contact with Connor, and join in the circle around our wolf. I hold my palms toward her and gasp. The woman's mouth looks like it's been sewn closed with thick, black thread. Normally a silencing spell would just keep someone from talking, but for whatever reason, Sascha decided to put a little more effort into this one.

The woman's eyes bulge, and her nostrils flare as she struggles to open her mouth. A wave of nausea hits me as Kelsey's voice echoes in my head.

Do you always torture your vics?

I hear the van door shut, and know Connor has headed back away from the scene.

Coward.

The second the thought pops into my head I immediately feel guilty, but the word lingers.

"Are we ready, people?" Margo yells.

I nod, wondering if everyone else was as stunned by Sascha's spell as I was.

"*Reveal!*" we all yell.

The ball of light forms over the woman's head. I fix my eyes on her face to see if the transformation will break the thread tying her mouth shut. Part of me hopes it does. Her face draws out into the snout of a wolf, and I see the string magically threading itself through her white fur to keep the new, longer mouth shut. I turn away as bile rises in my throat.

"Jules!" Dani yells.

I swallow and take out my gun. I turn back toward the wolf, aim at her heart, and fire.

The wolf's body flinches once, and blood stains the white fur. She starts to change back and I'm relieved to see the thread crumble and fall from her face.

Connor gets out of the van, and whistles a bit from a song as he lays the body bag next to her.

"Connor!" I say. "Stop that."

"What?" he asks looking puzzled.

"The whistling!"

"Oh, sorry, I forgot you have a soft spot for wolves."

"I don't have a soft spot—it's just, it's just disrespectful!"

He holds his hands up in the air in front of him. "Okay—sorry."

"Never mind that," Z says. "How is it you were the person the wolf was going to meet, and what the hell was up with your silencing spell, Sascha? That was a bit much, don't you think?"

"Yeah," Dani says softly. "Her mouth—it . . ." Dani brings her fingers up to her lips and doesn't finish her sentence.

Sascha looks around at all of us, visibly shaken. "I—I

didn't mean to do that—honest! I was so scared and it came out stronger than I'd wanted." She grabs the chain of her necklace with a shaking hand. "When I touched the stone I had a vision. It was horrible. I didn't want it to come true. I had to stop that lady from . . . " She turns to Margo. "Did you know I'd see the meetinghouse? Is that why you told me to hold it?"

"I wasn't sure if you'd be able to see anything, but I was hoping you would," Margo says. She sounds tired. "I wanted you to stop running at the mouth—so it wouldn't come true. All of us have to do exactly what we're supposed to—"

"Because if we don't," Sascha says, "one of us is going to Hell."

10

I shiver in the cold and wish the wind wasn't
sucking away all the heat from the small blaze we have going
in the campsite's fire-pit. We're all looking at Sascha, waiting
for her to talk, as the wood crackles and pops trying to warm
the night air.

"All I know," Sascha says, "is when I grabbed the stone
in the center of the necklace, I saw a demon in the meetinghouse—like it was right in front of me. And then everything speeded up and I only saw snatches of faces. I can't
even say who exactly was there because the whole thing was
over in a second or two. But there was a demon and it took
someone, that I'm sure of. I heard screaming and then I was
overwhelmed with a feeling of loss. I knew that someone

had messed up and someone had been taken." She bites her lower lip. "I could even smell brimstone."

I look at Connor on the other side of the fire. He fidgets his feet in the dirt and I wish I could apologize for snapping at him before. I wish he were sitting next to me, with his arms around me making me feel safe, instead of pretending we aren't together.

"Helena told me I had to keep the wolf from talking," Sascha continues. "After I had the vision, I was afraid if I didn't do what she'd said it might come true."

"Is that what you saw, too, Margo?" I ask. "The demon?"

Margo stares into the fire and nods. "Yeah," she says quietly. "I saw the same scene on my birthday during the ceremony. I noticed my necklace was glowing while Helena was talking. I reached down, and when my fingers touched the stone I saw the same thing. It took every ounce of energy I had not to scream because for a second I thought it was really happening. I looked at Helena and my mom to see if maybe they'd seen something, too, but they were going on like nothing happened.

"I can't tell you how many times I've held that necklace hoping to get a better glimpse—but it all flashes by so fast. I finally had to stop wearing it because I was driving myself crazy."

Margo reaches out and holds Sascha's hand and gives it a

squeeze. Dani and I exchange looks. I'm sure she's feeling as guilty as I am for what we'd said about Margo earlier.

Z clacks her tongue on her teeth. "So what does it mean?"

"Margo and Sascha's birthstones are supposed to enable the power of foresight," I say, "but I don't know if what they saw will definitely come true or not."

"We have to make sure it doesn't," Margo says. "We have to follow the rules."

"Damn," Z says. "Things are getting weirder and weirder, and now we have to worry about a demon snatching one of us."

"I'm scared," Dani whispers.

No one says anything. We watch the fire and I wonder if everyone is thinking what I am. Who will mess up and who will the demon take?

"What about you, Connor?" Z says, breaking the silence. "You still haven't told us why was the wolf coming up here to meet *you*?"

"Oh, well, she was trying to blackmail the coven," he says quickly, scratching his nose. "She found out about us and threatened to spread around who the hunters are—which could affect your safety. She offered us a price for her silence and we agreed." He folds his arms across his chest, and looks at the ground, kicking a rock toward the fire pit. "We set up the drop-off and you took care of our blackmailer."

My heart starts to pound faster than it already was. Connor's lying. Dani starts asking something, but I don't hear it. All I can hear is the word *liar* in my head. I wish I had the Ouroboros to prove I'm wrong, but his body language is telling me I'm not.

But why would he lie about the wolf?

"What if a bunch of wolves decided to hunt *you* before you could hunt *them*? They could catch you totally unprepared." I hear Connor say.

"Wow," Dani says. "To think about someone hunting us—I can't even imagine." She takes the flask from Zahara, takes a gulp, and is about to pass it to Sascha, but draws her hand back.

"I'll take a little," Sascha says, " . . . just to take the edge off." Dani gives it to her and she takes a long drink. She wipes her mouth on her sleeve and hands it to Connor. "I think it's safe to say we all need to be careful. Keeping our noses clean is the smartest, and really the only thing we can do right now."

Z shakes her head. "But this is freaking nuts!"

"There has to be something more you can tell us!" I say. "Do you even know how crazy this is for the rest of us?"

"Yeah," Z says. "With the way you two are acting, I gotta say I'm no longer looking forward to my birthday. I've grilled my mom a million times about all this shit, but she won't say a thing. I thought for sure we'd get some scoop from you guys."

Sascha sighs. "I wanted to tell you *some* stuff, but after that vision—I gotta side with Margo on this. I can't."

Margo scowls at her. "*You of all people* should have come to that conclusion at the initiation!"

Sascha hunches over and her long hair falls forward, hiding her face. "I know. I know," she says. "I was just so freaked out. And then I had a drink—or two." Her voice cracks and her shoulders shake. "It made it easier to pretend there was nothing to worry about—to pretend I didn't care."

"Well, look, it's only a couple more weeks until everyone's eighteen," Margo says, "and then we can decide as a group how we want to handle things. This coven has been living under a shadow for a long time, and it's about time someone did something about it."

"But my birthday isn't for another month!" I say.

"Be thankful," Sascha says.

"Just hang in there," Connor says, a little too cheerleader-y after what's just gone down. "It'll all work out." He stands and fishes the keys from his pocket. "It's really late. Let's pack it in, okay?"

Dani looks at her watch. "Two fifty! God, I'm so gonna bomb my quiz." She picks up her broom and then glances back at the fire. "Oh, we'd better not leave it going—it could spread or something."

"Always the Girl Scout," Margo mutters.

Dani gives an exasperated sigh. "Well, it could!" She points toward the fire. "*Out*!"

The fire sizzles and dies away, and I draw my cape closer to my body to capture some of the fading warmth.

Everyone else mounts their sticks, but I walk over to Connor.

"I'll help you with the body if you want," I say, trying to keep my voice without emotion, so it sounds like a casual offer. I catch the looks darting between Zahara and Margo. "It's really a two-person job," I add.

I hear Z clack her tongue. "Later."

Dani gives me a quick smile. "Bye!"

They take off. We watch them fade from view, and then Connor reaches out for my hand.

My first impulse is to pull it away, but his hand is warm, and I so want to be wrong about him.

"Thanks for helping," he says. "I wish it weren't so late— we could have some fun in the van."

I give him a horrified look. "The van? The one you cart dead bodies around in? And after everything that just happened?"

Connor laughs nervously. "Well, when you say it like that it doesn't sound so romantic."

"This isn't funny!" I snap, yanking my hand from his. "There's nothing funny about anything that happened tonight."

My breath comes out in fast steaming plumes as I stare into his shocked face.

"Why did you lie about the wolf?"

His eyes grow wide and then he looks away. "I had to."

"Why?" I ask, surprised and relieved he admitted it.

He takes my hand again and pulls me gently so I'm facing him. "Jules, there is so much going on, so much stuff you couldn't have imagined in your wildest dreams. I came up with an idea to try to fix things—fix things so we can make those changes we've talked about." He smiles a huge beaming smile. "And my mom's on board. Well, she doesn't know everything." He leans in and kisses me quickly.

I study his face—he looks excited and happy.

"But you're right about the wolf; she wasn't blackmailing the coven. She did know about us, though, and you know how dangerous that could be. That's all I can say right now. Can you trust me? For a little bit longer?"

"Connor, my head is absolutely spinning with all the secrets. I don't know what to think anymore."

Of course, I'm keeping secrets, too. Why haven't I told Connor about Evan and Finn? I look up at him and he gives me a lopsided grin.

"Just a little bit longer," he says again. He tilts my chin up and kisses me hard.

I push out all my worries and kiss him back hungrily.

"You're still coming over tomorrow after school, right?"

"Yeah," I say.

"Don't forget to bring the ring. I have to make sure it's back before it's missed."

"Where's your mom going to be anyway?"

"She's talking to some people about my idea—they wanted a face-to-face meeting." He smiles. "Cross your fingers, this could be what we're waiting for." He wraps me in his arms and spins me around.

"Don't make me wait too long," I laugh, breathless.

"Soon! I promise," he says.

We walk over to the woman's body. The cold breeze whips past me, and the lightness I just felt is carried off with it. I wonder if there's someone waiting for her at home. Did she tell a boyfriend or a husband she'd be back *soon*? I look down at her body—the torn clothes, the bullet hole leaking blood.

I did that to her.

I close my eyes and try to think back—past Kelsey—to the last time I'd felt more than a passing inkling of guilt after taking someone's life.

My mind is blank.

How many years have I have been immune from truly caring?

Wolves kill, I hear my mother say as we sat curled up on the couch when I was five. She held a witch ball in her hand. The bottom of the clear ball was covered with blue and purple spots of melted glass—my favorite colors. Inside the ball, the colored spots rose into thin glass threads where they connected with the top, ready to catch a spell.

Mom raised her hand and whispered, enchanting the ball. Yellow light swirled up and down the glass threads and finally a round moon appeared within the glass. **And if the wolf's victim should survive, the cycle of killing continues with each tortured full moon.**

I snuggled up closer to her, wondering what she meant by "tortured full moon." I reached out for the ball—holding it in my own small hand. The moon dissolved into a twinkle of stars. Each star stretched out tiny black wings and took the form of a bat. The bats flapped their wings, dipping and diving around the threads. **Vampires turn their victims into hollow, hungry creatures that prey on the living with an insatiable thirst.**

The bats disappeared as the ball filled with gray smoke. Two black eyes with pupils flickering fire appeared in the middle. I caught a glimpse of a piglike snout with long, curled teeth jutting out. My mother took the ball from my hand just as I was about to drop it.

Demons covet the human soul more then all the riches in

the world. They'll stop at nothing to bargain, trick, or deceive to get what we hold most precious. And that is why Mommy has to go out again tonight.

I looked past her toward the doorway where Cady Tompkins, who'd be watching me that night, stood.

And why someday, you will, too—*She paused and whispered a spell. The ball emptied and only my reflection—wide and distorted on the glass—shown.* **To keep the world safe.**

I jump at the sound of Connor unzipping the bag.

He's kneeling on the ground making the opening wider. "The easiest way to do it is to flip her onto the opening, and then work the limbs in."

"Right," I say, thinking this is the first time I've actually touched a dead body. I wonder if we have a cleanup crew so the hunters can remove ourselves from what we've just done.

"I'll take the top, you take the bottom. Ready?"

"I suppose." I kneel down, and the wet mud soaks into the knees of my jeans. I reach my hands under her hips. A shiver racks through me as I feel her cooling skin.

"You don't have to do this," he says. "You can go home and I'll take care of everything."

"No, I want to."

"Okay, then. One, two, three!"

I flip her over onto the bag and jump away as she lands

with a soft thud. A bigger, more violent shudder hits me, and I struggle to catch my breath. I watch Connor work her into the bag and then zip it up.

He looks up at me with sympathetic eyes. "If it makes you feel any better, I think this part is easier than what you have to do."

I look at the bag—blood smearing the inside.

"No. That doesn't make me feel any better."

11

Dani shuts her science book, and reaches across my kitchen table for a handful of popcorn from the bowl. "I can't concentrate on this. All I can think about is how I'm gonna wet my pants when they bring me into the back room of the meetinghouse in a few days!"

"Well, given what's been going down, I don't think even Margo could fault you for that," I say.

"Yeah, but I don't know if I can pretend I'm all excited going to the initiation knowing I'm about to learn some scary, ass-kicking, life-altering stuff. I always thought the initiation would be more like 'decide what you want to do for a coven job, so you can get trained before you retire from hunting.' Now I'm expecting Helena to say 'Screw up and you're demon chow!' Not exactly the happy birthday I was envisioning."

"We still don't know if that vision will come true, but I can pretty much guarantee we go on a hunt afterward. They seem to be testing the birthday girls directly after the initiations."

"Yeah," Dani says. "I was wondering about that. It's like they knock the crap out of you and then see if you're still up for the hunt. Can't wait to see what they have in store for me."

"You won't be alone. We'll be with you."

"Well, I'm glad we recharged our necklaces today—it makes me feel safer." Dani runs her fingers along the rim of Mom's spell bowl. "Oh! I told Evan I couldn't go out to dinner on my birthday, and he was totally okay with doing lunch instead. Of course, I'd much rather go out for a romantic dinner with him than get the 'your life will now suck' speech from Helena."

"Did you tell Evan why you couldn't go out to dinner?"

"Yeah, no! He hasn't even brought up the fact that I'm a witch, so I'm not about to tell him I have a coven initiation ceremony to attend instead of going out to eat with him."

"You haven't talked about it all? The way Finn was going on, I figured it was all out in the open."

"Are you sure Finn said Evan knows?"

I nod. "Positive."

"Well, he hasn't mentioned it once, and I haven't found a good time to talk about it. He's kind of shy, so I don't think he's going to ask me about it any time soon, either. Finn, on the other hand, grills me every time we're alone."

"About being a witch?"

"That, and he's totally hung up about what would happen if he boiled a fairy! The guy is beyond weird—like he could even see a fairy, let alone catch one! I think the only reason he and Evan are friends is because they live across the street from each other."

I laugh, thinking back to the conversation I had with Finn. "So, what did you tell him about the fairies?"

"I said until he tells me how he knew we were witches, I'm not telling him anything, and especially not how fairies punish someone who boils one of their kind." Dani looks at me and her cheeks flush. "Can I ask you something?"

"Anything."

She takes a deep breath and now her whole face is red. "I know you and Connor didn't exactly take things slow, but did *you* have to, like—you know—get things moving as far as, you know—what comes after first base?"

I shake my head and feel my cheeks flush, too. "Uh, no. We didn't have any problem moving past first base."

Dani slumps in her chair. "It's probably because I'm fat—he doesn't want to touch me."

"You're not fat! And Evan is just one of those really shy guys. I told you what Finn said about him, he's probably scared to make the first move." I give her a sly look. "But that doesn't mean you can't."

"I couldn't!" Dani says, eyes wide. "Could I?" We both laugh and then Dani bites her lower lip. "Sometimes I wish he were more like Finn."

"What? Why?"

"I really like Evan, but when I'm alone with Finn I laugh a lot, and I can talk about being a witch."

"You shouldn't be telling him stuff! And when are you alone with Finn?"

Dani cocks her head and raises one eyebrow. "Uh, that was *you* who told Finn stuff, not me! But when we're all hanging out at the library, Evan has to go blow his nose like every twenty minutes—it's kind of annoying, but since he's too embarrassed to do it in front of us he's always heading to the bathroom.

"As soon as Evan's out of sight Finn starts in. 'Do you prefer eye of newt or dried bat wings on your toast? Who cast the spell that turned Margo into a bitch?' That kind of stuff."

I laugh. "He sure has Margo's number down!"

"Yeah." Dani smiles for a second and then purses her lips. "But when it's just Evan and me we mostly talk about school and his robotics club, which isn't nearly as interesting as he thinks it is."

I smile at her sympathetically.

"I just feel like I can't totally be myself with him."

"You know—maybe not talking about the witch stuff with Evan *is* the problem," I say. "He knows, so if you can just get it out in the open, then you can both relax and have a little fun." I raise my eyebrows up and down and toss a piece of popcorn in my mouth.

"Yeah, you're right, but I just wish he'd bring it up first. Maybe after we go out to lunch I'll sit him down and we can talk. I'll have to tell my mom I'm heading to the library *again*. I told her it's easier to study there and she bought it. But it's hard sneaking around, you know?"

"Tell me about it."

Dani sighs. "At least *your* boyfriend is in the coven." She leans in toward me and raises her eyebrows. "So, do *you* have any big plans for today? What time are you heading over to his—"

Mom walks in from outside, and Dani stops mid-sentence.

"Hi, girls," she says brightly.

I stop myself before I roll my eyes. It's getting harder and harder to tolerate her Pollyanna-sunshiny act when I know she'll be dumping some horrific secret on me in a few weeks.

But maybe having been through the same thing when she was my age, she figures if she got through it, so will I.

"Hi, Mrs. Harris," Dani says without her usual enthusiasm.

Mom puts a box on the table in front of us. "Want to see what I've been working on?" She takes out two glass balls, and gives one to each of us. Immediately I see they're different from her normal witch balls. Instead of several fine glass threads rising up from the bottom of the ball, there are only two in these, almost half an inch thick. The walls of the orbs are thicker, too—and she used a dull, brown glass, very different from the brightly colored balls she usually makes.

"Uh, hate to say it, but it's not your best work," I say. "They're kind of dreary."

Mom puts her hands on her hips. "They have to be made this way. It's a special configuration . . ." She pauses and breaks out in a big smile. "To capture ghosts!"

Mom's looking at us with wide-eyed expectation, but Dani and I exchange puzzled looks.

"Why would you want to *capture* a ghost?" I ask.

"Yeah," Dani says. "I thought the whole point of going after ghosts was to help them move on or to exorcise them if they're nasty and need a little nudge in the right direction."

Mom sits down at the head of the table and holds her hand out to me. I give her the ball and she brings it up to the light. "You don't think it would be interesting to contain a ghost in one of these?"

"Uh, interesting how?"

"You could actually own a ghost!"

I look at Mom smiling, her eyes still wide and excited, and shake my head. "I guess I'm missing something, because I'm not finding anything appealing about trapping the spiritual entity of a person in a ball. Besides, what would any of us do with a ghost? And what fun would it be for the ghost to just have a small ball to haunt?"

"Well, I don't know that a ghost has much fun haunting a house," Mom says. "They seem rather tortured about it. But perhaps it would be a relief for them to be removed from whatever was keeping them among the living."

"I think it'd be more tortured being cooped up in a tiny glass ball," I reply.

"Well, I can kind of see how it might be neat," Dani says. "Like if you had the ghost of someone famous you could show it off at parties."

"What?" I say.

Dani shrugs. "Well, like, it would be a conversation starter."

"Exactly!" Mom says. "You'd own a ghost—one of a kind. And there are plenty of people who'd love to add a ghost to their list of collectibles."

"Sure, a ghost ball would look great next to someone's shrunken head collection," I say.

Mom shakes her head and puts the ball back in the box. "I've been working on them for two days straight and thought you'd be a little more excited about this."

I take the other ball from Dani's hand and hold it up to

the light like Mom did, hoping to find something alluring. I shake my head. "Do they have to be brown? I mean even if I did want a pet ghost, the color kind of sucks."

Dani kicks me under the table. "I think it's a cool idea."

"And what do *you* think of the brown color?" Mom asks her.

Dani tilts her head back and forth looking at the ball in my hand. "Uh, it's okay. I guess. Does it *have* to be brown?"

"Actually," Mom says looking defeated, "they're supposed to be blue, but every time I combine the reveal spell with a retrieval spell, the glass goes mud-colored on me." She takes the ball from me and puts it in the box with the other. "Well, I guess it's back to the workshop to see if I can make some blue balls."

This time I kick Dani, and we both look away, giggling.

"You know," Mom says, "before I make too many, it sure would be nice to see if the basic design works. Are you girls doing anything now?"

"Mom," I moan, thinking Connor is expecting me soon. The last thing I want to do is go ghost busting. "I have studying to do. We were going to the library because we can't concentrate here!"

"It won't take too long—just a quick trip to the Fayetteville border. There's the remains of an old brewery—"

"The High Tower Brewery?" Dani asks. "I heard some kids

at school talking about it—people go and dare each other to enter the ruins at midnight. Rob Walsh said *something* tried to claw his eyes out when he went, but everyone thought he was bullsh—uh, I mean, making it up."

Mom smiles and nods. She can see Dani is interested, so she's probably thinking I'll go along with this, too.

"Well, the young man might not have been exaggerating," she says. "The brewery lost over twenty people in a fire set by a disgruntled employee. We have it on good authority that some victims lingering on the spot could be classified as poltergeists. You girls can go and give the balls their first test. If the new configuration of the threads and the enchantment we put on them works, you'll come home with two ghosts!"

"You mean two former employees who died a horrible death," I say, folding my arms across my chest, "who probably don't want to become someone's pet ghost."

"They're poltergeists—and angry ones at that. You'd be making the place safer."

"If it's so dangerous, why haven't we cleaned it up before?"

Mom gives me the exasperated sigh I'm hearing more and more lately. "It hasn't been a top priority because we prefer to use our resources on the creatures that kill."

"Yeah," Dani says, "if we're going to go hunting it's better to go after something that could perpetuate the cycle, and while a poltergeist could knock you around a bit it wouldn't . . ." She sees me giving her an utterly bored look and pauses. "Well, you know—kill you."

"Fine!" I say, holding out my hand. Mom smiles and gives me the ball back. "If you want a ghost that badly I'll get you one. Consider it an early Christmas present."

"That's my girl. All you have to do is hold the ball in one hand and then when you use the reveal spell, instead of the ghost just appearing so you could exorcise it, it'll become trapped in the ball. Well, if it works."

"Whatever," I say. "I'll get some binders and whatnot just in case something else is hanging around, but then we're going to the library where we won't be interrupted!"

Mom tilts her head. "Funny how studious you're getting all of a sudden."

I've been waiting for her to say something like this, but I'm prepared. "Well, after you totally *embarrassed* me in front of Mrs. Keyes, I thought I should try a little harder to get my grades up. Speaking of which, should we drop the ghost balls at Mrs. Keyes's house?" I ask.

Dani smirks and I give her a sideways look to knock it off.

"No, bring them back here—Helena's out of town for a bit."

"Oh, I didn't know. We'll bring them back here then, before we go to the library."

I get up and put on my cape. I place the ball carefully in my pocket, and Dani and I grab our brooms.

"Ghost balls," I mutter as we walk out into the crisp late afternoon sun. What a stupid idea!

We clear the house on our brooms, and Dani laughs out loud. "*Oh, I didn't know!*" she says, imitating me. "You're a pro at deception."

"Yeah, I thought that was a nice touch." I scan the ground. "Once we get to the river, how far is the brewery?"

"A couple of miles."

We fly in silence and I think about how weird it feels riding sticks in the daylight—even if I am cloaked. I close my eyes and feel the slight warmth from the late October sun on my face. I keep my broom steady and imagine the sun slanting through the window in Connor's room. I picture myself in his room—in his bed.

"Jules!" Dani yells.

My eyes snap open. "What?"

"We're almost there." She points down toward the shell of an old brick building with a tall, thin maple tree sporting bright red and orange leaves sprouting out through an opening in the roof.

I clutch my broom tightly, and we circle the building and land along the riverbank sending up a flurry of dead leaves. I

look up at the old tower—the one thing that's still intact—
and make out the High Tower Brewery letters barely visible
after years of neglect.

We stand there listening and watching for any sign that
some other creatures may have set up camp here. Some things
like to hang in haunted places to avoid unwanted contact
with humans, not counting the drunken teenagers that may
crash their lairs now and again at night, but in the midday
they'd probably be lying low.

I don't hear anything other than squirrels foraging in the
trees that are growing right up to the sides of the building, but
there's a definite electric feel to the air typical of the energy
poltergeists let off.

"Creepy-crawly feeling alert," I say.

"Yeah," Dani agrees. "I don't think this will be like that last
ghost we dealt with—the little girl—the one who was looking
for her mother."

"Only the mother had been dead for like a hundred years!
She wasn't so bad, except for the pinching part."

"And the hair pulling."

I laugh. "Hey, give ghost-girl props for kicking Margo in
the ass, that was too funny! But still, once we started with the
exorcism she didn't put up too much of a fight." I cross my
arms over my chest as the air temperature drops dramatically.
"I have a feeling there's definitely more than one ghosty here,

though." I take the ball out of my pocket. "Let's get this over with. I have to be at Connor's soon."

Dani nods and we carefully pick our way among the roots and empty beer and soda cans along the building's edge until we find an open doorway. We walk through and I shudder as a crop of goose bumps breaks out on my arms. There's plenty of sunlight pouring through the broken windows and holes in the walls and ceilings, but the temperature keeps dropping.

Suddenly a brick flies at our heads. Dani and I duck and it sails past us and crashes against the wall. Another brick slams into a window above us. We run farther into the room to avoid the glass raining down.

"I don't think the inhabitants are happy to see us," I say.

"I hope they're not face warpers," Dani says, wrapping her cape tighter. "I hate it when they get all freaking weird and give themselves long teeth and crap like that; it gives me nightmares. I mean why do they have to do that anyway?"

I hold two fingers up like sharp fangs. "All the better to eat you with, my dear."

Dani punches me in the arm.

"Ow, what did you do that for?"

"You're creeping me out!"

An old ceramic tile pulls up from the floor and aims straight for our heads. "*Stop!*" I yell, and hold my palm toward it. The tile shatters before it gets to us, but then the broken pieces swirl up together and come at us like a swarm of bees.

We turn and hold our capes up to protect our faces. I wince as the pieces rocket into my back and then clatter to the ground. "Let's do this before we get hurt!" I yell.

Dani nods. She takes out the witch ball from her pocket, and we stand back-to-back. The brewery is oddly still and I wonder if the ghosts have all stopped their fun to see what we're up to.

"*Reveal!*" we both yell.

I gasp as at least a dozen shadowy bodies appear around us in a circle. Their smoky faces—charred and blistered, some down to their spectral cheekbones—stare at us with wide empty eyes. They hover around us for another second and then the witch ball in my hand vibrates. As if sensing a change, they all start to zip off in different directions, but I see one ghost being drawn toward the ball. The ghost stretches out longer and longer as it tries to get away, but a piece of it makes contact with the ball. In a flash of blinding light, it disappears, and then I see a faint green light pulsing around inside—winding its way around the glass threads.

"I got one!" I say turning to Dani.

"Me, too," she says, holding out her ball.

We watch the lights pulse and wane, and then a burnt

mouth presses itself against the inside of Dani's ball. Its blistered tongue probes the glass for a second before dissolving back into an eerie green light. "Ew!" she says. "I've changed my mind about having a pet ghost!"

A loud crash bangs in the next room and I jerk my head toward the door. "Let's get out of here!"

I grab Dani's hand, and we run through the room. I hear a tinkle of falling glass behind us as we cross the threshold into the woods. More crashes and strange noises echo out after us as we stumble through the leaves and undergrowth until we find our brooms. We run toward the river and then sit at the edge of the bank.

"You know—after all that," I pant, "I don't feel so bad about trapping one of these things!" I pick up a rock and toss it into the dark water.

Dani frowns and then pockets her witch ball in her cape. She looks over to me and sighs. "Evan and I are never going to be together, are we?"

"What? Of course you are. You're together now."

Dani shakes her head. "No, not really." She sniffs and brushes a tear away. "You said I should talk to him about what it means to be a witch, right? Well, if I told him what just went down he'd probably throw up." She waves an arm back at the brewery. "And this is freaking tame compared to most of the things we do."

"Give him a chance, Dani. Talk to him when you go out to lunch."

"We slaughtered two people this week, do I fit that into the conversation before or after dessert?"

We stare at each other, our breath frosting in the air. I know she's right, but I don't want to admit it out loud.

"I don't know, but don't give up on Evan without at least trying. Here," I say, holding my hand out. "I'll take both balls back. Go home, put on that skirt you like, and get ready to meet him at the library. When the time is right, you can tell him everything and give him a chance to accept you—the real you."

Dani's shoulders slump and then she picks up her broom. "I wish the real me didn't have anything to tell."

Several bricks come flying out of a broken window of the brewery, and thud in the dead leaves a few feet behind us. Dani shakes her head sadly. "I think I want to fly home alone. Do you mind?"

"No, go ahead."

I take the witch ball from her and she mounts her broom. She gives me a half smile and heads up. A loud moan emits from the ball in my hand. I grimace and stuff it into my other pocket. The balls rattle and jump in my cape, and one ghost lets out a long plaintive howl.

Yeah, catching ghosts was a stupid idea.

So is dating people outside the coven.

I wish it weren't true, but I know Dani was right. Evan isn't the kind of guy who would be okay with all of this.

I mount my stick and head home, thanking God that Connor is.

12

I double around Connor's house to check if his mom's car is gone. With no sign of her black Mercedes, I head down to the backyard.

My body warms, imagining myself in his arms with no worries about our moms.

I land by the back door and knock. Footsteps get louder, and Connor pulls back the lace curtain covering the window in the door. I rush past him into his kitchen and uncloak.

"I almost thought you weren't going to come," he says as he shuts the door.

I slip into his arms and let him kiss me hard. "Mmmmm." I kiss him again. I dance out away from him and take off my cape.

Connor looks me up and down. "But it was worth the wait."

I smile and blush. "My mom ambushed me before I could leave. I had to test out a new witch ball for her."

"Did you catch a ghost?" he asks, eyes wide.

"Yeah," I say surprised. "How did you know?"

"It's part of my plan." Connor grins and then he bites his lip like he's trying really hard to decide something. "I have to tell you—I can't hold it in any longer." He grabs my hand and leads me up the stairs.

"Where are we going?" I ask.

"To that room I was telling you about."

My heart revs up a bit. I wasn't sure if he would show me the room. At the very least, I imagined I was going to have to do some begging!

He leads me up the dark stairwell. I've never been upstairs before and I shake my head at the rust-colored paint. I'm about to roll my eyes, thinking it was just like Helena to pick such a morbid color, but maybe it's left over from the previous coven leader. Connor's house is one of the original coven houses from after our third move, and the narrow halls and low ceilings start to make me feel claustrophobic.

When we get to the top I look down the long skinny hall, wondering which room is his and if the secret room might be hidden behind a bookcase or something.

"It's down at the end," he says. "I shouldn't be showing you, but I have to share this with someone, and . . ." He squeezes my hand. "You're the someone."

I follow him into a large room with bare walls. A single bed and desk sit under the eaves. A small silver bell sits on the desk, but otherwise the room is empty. Connor turns to me and the excitement in his eyes makes me smile despite the fact I'm not seeing anything all that interesting.

I look around, trying to figure out what's got him all jacked up. "I thought there would be some *stuff* in here," I say, my eyes darting around for something to get excited about, too.

Connor laughs. "Use the reveal spell."

"Oh," I say, finally understanding what he means. "The room isn't hidden, the stuff is."

He nods and I hold my palms out and then slowly walk in a circle. "*Reveal!*"

The room shimmers and sparkles and then I see everything—walls covered with shelves and cabinets and boxes. Several tables are brimming with all sorts of statuary and articles of clothing. Two long desks with thick, carved legs—one with a computer and scanner on it, now sit where the bed and small desk were. I notice the silver bell is now next to the mouse pad.

"There must be hundreds of things in here," I say, walking around, "maybe *thousands*. And what are these?" I say, pointing to a pair of long, twisted horns mounted on a piece of highly polished wood. "They don't belong on top of any animal head I've ever seen."

"I haven't identified them yet," Connor says. "But it's a safe bet they're demon. I e-mailed a photo to a demonologist to see if she can place what class of demon and what realm of Hell they might be from." Connor holds out his hands to his side. "So what do you think?"

I see a pair of fuzzy fur mittens and resist the urge to pick them up. After what happened with the Ouroboros, I know it's not safe to randomly examine anything in here. "Honestly, I don't know what to think. Is this all stuff we've collected from hunts?"

"Yeah, three hundred or so odd years worth of stuff. Some of which are the only remnants of the coven after the big fire in the 1800s. Everything in here is covered by a series of protective spells to keep it safe.

"But here's the deal—I'm in the middle of cataloging everything, and then we're going to start *auctioning* things off. My mom cast a spell on the bell. I just have to ring it, and the room reveals for me so I can work when she's not here."

"Your big plan is to sell all of this?" I ask, wondering how selling a few things is going to bring on any great change in the coven.

"Not all of it—some of it we have to save, but once I have

a picture and description for everything, the inner circle—which will include you very soon . . ." He smiles at me like I should be totally stoked about this, and I'm wondering if he's forgotten what Margo and Sascha said last night. ". . . will go through and decide what to keep and what to sell. But Jules, we could possibly make millions with the things in here."

I shake my head. "Do you really think the typical eBay shopper is gonna be looking for things like demon horns or, or—vests with enchanted eyes?"

"Oh, the *Maiden's Vest*! There are actually some people very interested in it. It's a great story. It's uh, very old—Northern European in origin. A group of young seers were brought to a temple in the Carpathian Mountains, faced out in different directions, and then bound in place. Some sort of ceremony took place, and their eyes were plucked out and sewn onto the vest. Whoever is wearing the vest can see what they *see*."

My eyes widen, wondering just what's so *great* about this story.

"I tried it on, and it's not just the surrounding mountains you can see." He shakes his head and gives me a "kid in the candy store" look. "You can cast the sight out as far as you want in any direction and see anything around the world. I actually was able to get a glimpse of you!"

Connor's face is flushed with excitement, but a creeping

sense of dread fills me. "You actually put that thing on and spied on me?"

"Jules! I wasn't spying on you, but I had to try the vest on to see if it still worked, and you were the first person that came to mind! But the woman who helped me dig up the info contacted some people who are willing to pay big bucks for that baby. And none of this is going on eBay—we have several auction companies that deal with supernatural items interested in representing the coven."

I look around the room some more and focus on some of the items. A shield propped up against the wall on a table that emits a bluish light sits next to a small replica of the Statue of Liberty. I lean in for a closer look, and see fangs on Lady Liberty. I notice the fur mittens have small mouths with tiny, razor-sharp teeth sticking out. Next to the mittens is a purple-and-blue wool hat, and I immediately think how warm it would be to wear it flying home later tonight. "That's not anything weird, is it?" I ask, pointing to the hat. It looks so soft and I'm overwhelmed with the desire to pick it up and put it on.

"Make it reveal," he says.

I put my palm above it. "*Reveal.*" The wool hat morphs into a plain brown derby.

"It's an ugly, old-man's hat." I look at Connor. "I'll bet you get top dollar for that one!"

"The hat assumes the shape of something the viewer would want to put on. To me it always looks like a Yankees cap. But if you put it on it'll clamp down on your head . . ." Connor pauses. "Until your skull is crushed," he says quietly.

"Lovely." I close my eyes for a few seconds and try to get the horrific image I've just conjured out of my mind.

I walk over to the desk and I'm about to pull out the chair to sit but turn to Connor. "Will the chair arms reach up and strangle me if I try to sit on it?"

Connor frowns. He's obviously picked up on the fact that I'm more disturbed than excited about his new venture. "No."

I pull the chair out and swivel to face him. "Do you really think it's a good idea sending some of these things back out into the world?"

"It's not all evil stuff—there's a ring that . . ."

"Bites its own tail. I've experienced that one firsthand, remember?"

Connor squeezes his eyes shut and sighs. "There's a ring," he starts again, "that makes the wearer feel more confident, and there's a small metal statue of a nightingale that sings beautiful songs. There's a lot of stuff in here that isn't bad."

"But you *were* planning on selling the very charming *Maiden's Vest* though, right?"

"Only if you all okay it," Connor says, all traces of

excitement gone from his voice. "*You're* in charge. I was just trying to find a way to contribute—to stop being dead weight around here."

How did we cross over into this territory again? "You're not dead weight! Look, I know you're excited about this new auction thing, but I'm just afraid selling some of these things would put the people we're trying to protect at risk."

"Well, there are a few kinks to work out before we're sure what we can try to sell, anyway, but it's the ghost balls we'll start out with."

"Was that *your* idea?" I ask, hoping the answer is no.

He nods and furrows his brows. He's probably worried I'm going to jump down his throat about them. I guess I can't really blame him—I seem to be doing that a lot lately.

"I uh, heard my mom talking with your mom. They were trying to figure out some, you know, stuff and they got to talking about the witch balls. I wondered aloud if they could trap a spell in it, then why not a ghost? They did some research and as you saw today—you can."

"How much would someone pay for a ghost, do you suppose?" I ask.

The corners of his mouth turn up ever so slightly. "Thousands of dollars. We already have a waiting list of people who've expressed an interest."

I imagine some rich, old crackpot showing off one of the

charred spirits I'd trapped today. Even though the ghosts were on the nasty side, I get a sick feeling about treating them like some sort of commodity to be sold off to the highest bidder.

"Besides the fact that there's something kind of twisted about selling someone's ghost," I say, "do we really need the extra money?"

Connor turns away from me and opens a small drawer in a cabinet. "Don't you ever want more?" he asks quietly.

"No—not more—different. We have everything we need living off the interest from the coven's savings. No one has to work really, so why would I want more?"

"It's a little more complicated than that," he says, opening and closing different drawers. "Look, how about we do something else?" He turns back to me. "Let's stow the Ouroboros away and then I can show you my room." He puts his head down and shrugs his shoulders. "If you still want to see it, that is."

My stomach flips uncomfortably at the disappointed tone of his voice. I've hurt him because I can't muster up the enthusiasm for all of this auction stuff—especially since I know he was hoping this venture would make him something other than the stereotypical coven grunt.

"I *do* want to see it," I say, walking toward him. I give him a half smile. "But you'll have to find the ring yourself." I walk over to him and put my arms around his shoulders. "I've got it wrapped up and hidden somewhere." I lick my lips. "You'll have to figure out where, though."

Connor grins and draws me close to him. "I love you so much, Jules." He nuzzles my neck and reaches his hands into my back pockets.

I hug him tighter. "I—I love you, too," I whisper, my heart racing.

He nibbles on my earlobe and moves his hands up under the back of my shirt, along my bra.

I kiss him gently. "You're getting warmer." I step back and Connor smiles hungrily.

He looks down at the front of my shirt and slowly slides a hand into my cleavage. I shiver as he brushes up against the small the ring taped up tightly in paper, pulls it out, and laughs. "You sure wrapped this up well," he says.

"I didn't want it biting me—especially there!"

"Am I allowed to?" he asks. He looks at me with half-closed eyes.

I lick my lips. "Maybe."

Connor puts the ring down on the table. "I'll take care of this later," he says. "I think you'll like my room a lot better than this one." He takes my hand and I'm certain tonight will be the night.

* * *

I lay next to Connor, watching his chest rise and fall in the moonlight. His eyes move back and forth beneath his lids and I wonder if he's dreaming about making love to me.

I hate that he won't.

You know it's not safe—even with protection. There are other things we can do.

I slip my feet out of bed and slowly pull on my underwear and pants. I search the floor for my bra, hook it on, and then tug my shirt over my head. It's just after nine. The library closed half an hour ago. I hope Mom is still out in her shop trying to keep the blue balls blue. I look at Connor and roll my eyes.

I put on my shoes and cringe as the floorboards squeak under my feet. Connor sighs in his sleep and I quietly shut his door.

I want one more look at the *auction* room. I step slowly down the hall and open the door. The glamour is back in place.

"*Reveal*," I whisper.

The room changes again. I walk along the far wall, looking at a row of knives and swords arranged neatly in a row on a table. One long thin saber moves, looking sharp and menacing as its tip follows me as I walk past. I hold my hand out ready to cast a spell if it decides to come flying off the table toward me.

I walk past the computer desk. It's clean and clutter-free, and given the state of Connor's room, I'm thinking Helena is the neat freak. I look at the spiral notebook with the word NOTES written in Connor's handwriting on the front. A thick, leather-bound book is underneath it. I move the notebook aside, and see LEDGER engraved on the worn black cover. I sit in the chair and open the book toward the beginning.

July 7, 1895 Vampire—female, blonde hair,
lithe of limb
July 10, 1895 Wolf—young male, perhaps eighteen,
tall, red hair, freckles
July 25, 1895 Shape-Shifter—male/mongrel, dog—
brown and black. 1,000 extra pieces
Much thanks to you—
And you in return.

That's weird. It looks like two people are writing in the book. I hope the second person was using brown ink and not blood to write in. I turn toward the middle of the book.

December 24, 1945—three wolves, all male
December 30, 1945—wolf, retrieved pendant. Keep
pendant with the others, 5,000 extra

Thank you
January 4, 1946 — vampire, female

I flip through page after page of dates and records. The recorder has obviously changed as the years have passed, and so have the details they chose to include with each kill, but the brown handwriting scattered here and there remains consistent. How is that possible?

I turn toward the back. Let's see what Helena's written in here.

"Jules! What are you doing?"

I slam the book shut and jump up. "Connor," I say. "God, you scared me! I just wanted another look around."

He's standing in the doorway in his boxers. "You shouldn't be here alone and it's getting late."

"This book," I say, laying a hand across it. "Do you know there's a record of all of the kills ever made? Have you ever looked through it?"

"No," he says, rubbing his eyes. "I leave that stuff to my mom, but like I said, it's late. You should probably head home before your mom starts to worry—and ask questions."

"Yeah." I push the chair back and Connor holds out his hand. I take it, and as I walk out, I look back into the room and see it's already hidden its secret stash.

"Could I come back tomorrow? I'd really like to spend

some more time looking through that book again."

I feel Connor stiffen. "I don't think that's a good idea, I'm not sure when my mom will be back. But I'll let you know the next time I'm sure she'll be away."

"Great," I say, but I get the feeling he doesn't mean it. I shake my head to chase that thought away.

He walks me to the door and I see him shivering as I wrap my cape around myself.

"You should've put some clothes on, it's freezing in here."

He takes me in his arms and hugs me tight. "You're all the warmth I need."

"Uh-huh," I say. I kiss him and then tilt my head toward the stairs. "Get back to bed. I'll see you tomorrow."

As I head up over his house on my broom I see the light to the treasure room turn on. I swoop back down and hover by the window at what I hope is a safe distance so he won't see me. The room is revealed, but Connor's back is to me as he sits at the desk. The computer is booting up, and he unwraps the Ouroboros and drops it in a small wooden box.

He picks up a piece of paper and unfolds it. I can just make out a picture of the ring on the top of the page. The page is full of writing and I'm thinking there's a lot more information about the ring than Connor let on.

I shake my head. Why do I keep getting so worked up

about things? Connor isn't the one I need to worry about. He keeps showing me time and time again he wants nothing more than for us to be together—and to prove himself.

I lean away from the window and steer my broom toward home. If I'm looking for something to worry about, it should be how I can help Dani get through her birthday initiation in two days. She's already a basket case—I can't imagine she'll be much better after Helena welcomes her to the inner circle.

13

I wake from a dream of being chased on my broom by bricks with wings, and look at the clock—2:10 A.M. Figures it's quiet the one night I decide to wear my jeans to bed so I'd be ready for a hunt. I guess my theory about using hunts as an initiation test is a bust—none of the other birthday hunts have been this late and Dani's ceremony should have been over hours ago.

The kitchen light I left on for Mom is still glowing under my doorway.

I pull the covers up over my shoulders and nestle deeper into my pillow. I hope my mom stayed late to talk ghost balls or something, and Dani's home and in bed, too.

Poor Dani—she was so shaky and twitchy while Helena was doing her "now you're a woman" shtick. And she couldn't stop looking around the room all bug-eyed, like she was expecting the demon from Margo and Sascha's vision to pop up at any moment and drag her down to Hell.

At least I'll get some scoop tomorrow—Dani promised she'd tell me whatever she could that didn't violate whatever nonsense that was keeping Margo and Sascha from talking. We figured there's always a way to get around rules, and she'd continue her under-the-radar rebellion by telling me what I was in for.

We didn't get to talk about her lunch with Evan. Her mom was stuck to her side all night before the ceremony, and I couldn't get her alone to ask how it went. I did hear her mother bragging about Dani's grades and how seriously she's taking school—studying all the time. Hopefully she and Evan were able to talk and things were back on track.

I want to tell Dani about Connor's connection with the ghost balls, too. I don't know why I didn't tell her yesterday at school. Maybe I didn't because I'm still not sure how I feel about it.

I can see why Connor wants to do something to prove himself. And growing up in a coven, it's not a huge surprise he thought about making money off the supernatural. But I'd always hoped we'd break away and do something new, not stay and deal in the same old nightmares. I picture the Maiden's Vest and the old brown hat—you can't get more nightmarish than them. Even the Ouroboros is cute in comparison.

I let out a long sigh and roll over onto my stomach, thinking I've gotten too worked up to fall asleep again.

I hear the kitchen door open. Mom's finally home.

"Jules?"

That sounded like Dani. I sit up in bed, wondering if I was dreaming.

"Jules!"

It *is* her.

I pull my covers off and rush out of my room. "Dani?" I call out.

When I reach the top of the stairs I see Dani in the kitchen. Her face is red and puffy from crying. "Oh, my God! What happened?" I ask as I race down.

Dani rushes over and throws her arms around me. "She cast a spell," she sobs. "My own mother cast a spuh—" Dani chokes on her words and holds me tighter.

"What? A spell?"

Dani pulls back and her lower lip quivers. "It's horrible! We, we're—uh—"

"What? Tell me what happened."

Her face crumples. "I can't," she cries. "My mother cast a spell on me! I told them I was going to tell you and Zahara, and Helena—uh, made her do it."

"They cast a spell on you so you wouldn't tell us what?"

Dani shakes her head. "Don't you understand? I can't freaking tell you!" Her face is flushed and her eyes are wild. "But we have to get away—we have to leave. We can't do this to—uh." Dani shakes her head as if she's trying to shake the spell away. "Damn them!" she screams.

I stare at her not sure what to do. I want to get behind her anger, but I don't know what to be angry about. "Okay, slow down and tell me what you can."

Dani bites her lip and sits at the kitchen table. I take the seat opposite from her and hold my hand out. She reaches for it, and squeezes it tight.

"It's totally unreal what they did—we always thought we were—uh." Dani looks up at the ceiling and growls with frustration. "We have to get Margo and Sascha to tell you, we have to stop this from—uh." She slams her fist on the table. "God, I hate them!"

"Wait, if you can't tell me what happened, maybe I can guess. Do you think you could nod yes or no?"

Dani shakes her head. "Jules, you'd never guess what we're up against, not in a million years." Her bottom lip quivers and tears roll down her cheeks.

"Does it have to do with the demon?"

Dani rolls her eyes. "Tip of the iceberg," she says slowly.

I take a deep breath. Demons are the *tip* of the iceberg? How bad will this get?

"Okay, is it if someone talks or breaks one of the rules the demon will come?"

"I'm not sure—but we wuhhh-uh for uhh—" She buries her face in her hands. "How could Margo and Sascha be okay with this?" she whispers.

"I don't think they are, they—"

"They didn't fight it!" Dani yells. "They just sucked it up. But I know you'll be on my side. We'll find a way to stop it. Or we have to leave—hide—get away from here."

The kitchen door opens and we both jump. Our mothers walk in, with Helena trailing behind.

"Honey, we've been looking all over for you," Mrs. Robbins says, rushing over to us.

"Don't touch me!" Dani yells.

Mrs. Robbins stops a few feet away from us. Her face is white and drawn, and her eyes are almost as red and puffy as Dani's. "Thank you for looking after her, Julia," she says, forcing a too-big smile on her face.

"How could you do it to her?" I ask, looking Mrs. Robbins in the eye.

Mrs. Robbins's hand flutters to her chest nervously, and she looks back at Mom for a second. "I—I didn't have a choice. Did I, Catherine?"

"There's always a choice," I say. "And you caved in and silenced your own daughter with a spell."

Mom stands by Mrs. Robbins' side. "Julia!"

"Oh, sorry!" I say, getting up and walking over to Dani. I put my hands on her shoulders and feel her shaking. "I mean just because you've kept a huge, God-awful secret from us all these years doesn't mean we should get all pissy about it. What *were* we thinking?"

"But she couldn't have told you," Mrs. Robbins says with wide eyes. She turns to Helena. "You saw me cast the spell."

"Yeah, don't worry, your spell works just fine," I say. "But I'm not an idiot. It's obvious you all have been covering up something rotten. I guess Dani was just the first one with the balls to say *enough is enough*."

"Yes, Julia. Enough is enough," Helena says, her voice calm, but dripping with venom. She walks slowly toward the table, looking around the kitchen with a serene look on her face.

She turns her gaze to me, and her icy eyes lock onto mine. I feel my confidence ebbing, but I don't look away.

"It's hard for you girls to wait for your birthday," she says. "And I know you're aware you have some very grown-up decisions to make—the same ones your mother made, and all of the hunters that came before her did as well."

She walks closer to me, and I can't help but back away from Dani. Dani doesn't react—she just keeps staring down at her hands resting on the table, but I feel like I've abandoned her.

"I understand your frustration—really I do," Helena continues. "But don't for one second presume to know more than your elders. And as for you . . ." She reaches out and strokes Dani's hair. Dani doesn't flinch or move—it's like she's frozen into place. "You just need a little time to take in everything."

Dani's mom hurries over and takes Dani's hand. She gently tugs her up. Dani moves like a zombie—stiffly and without emotion. Mrs. Robbins wraps her arm around her, and they walk out without another word.

Helena gives me an evil victory smirk. "I know your initiation will run a bit smoother. You know what you want—and I think you know what you have to do to get it." She turns and her silver scarf falls off one shoulder and drags on the floor through the cat hair we haven't swept up.

I'm tempted to ignore it, but I know what she just said was a reference to Connor and me. A warning that if I want to be with him I'm going to have to kiss ass and be a good witch. I take a deep breath and exhale. "Your scarf is dragging," I say as sweetly as possible.

Helena turns and looks at me over her shoulder. "Why, thank you, Julia." She coils the scarf up around her neck and I wish I knew a spell that would turn it into a snake.

"Don't worry about Dani," Helena says. "She's a little more sensitive then the rest of you girls, but she'll come around. There really isn't any choice." She smiles broadly at me and then tips her head at Mom. "We'll talk in the morning, Catherine. Let me know if anything comes up."

"Of course," Mom says, and bile rises in my throat.

Helena shuts the door, and I head toward the stairs not wanting to have another "just wait" conversation.

"Julia!" Mom calls out. "We need to talk."

"Unless you plan on telling me the big birthday reveal, I'm going to bed," I say as I keep going.

"Don't you think I'd tell you if I could?" Mom says with a cracked voice.

I look up the stairs and focus on my door. "You need to tell me why I should stay instead of running off with Dani. I trust her, and unless you have something good to say, I have no problem hitting the road with her before my birthday."

"I'll tell you what I can," she says quietly.

I hear her pull a kitchen chair out. It creaks under her weight, and I turn and walk back to the table. I sit across from her but keep my gaze toward the cauldron bubbling on the stovetop.

"There's a covenant—a *magical* covenant that binds us to certain . . . protocols." She takes a deep breath. "But we don't have the actual paper that details the agreement anymore."

I give her an incredulous look. "You lost a magical contract?"

"It was a long time ago—one of the hunters decided she

didn't want to live under the covenant's restriction, so she burned the parchment along with a few of the coven houses."

"I take it that wasn't the end of the covenant?" I ask.

"No. The witch mistakenly assumed that simply destroying the paper the covenant was written on would void it—not thinking the other party involved still had their copy. The witch continued her reckless behavior, though. But then she discovered that the penalty for doing so was the life of a loved one."

I can't help but wonder if a demon was involved, but don't say anything about Margo and Sascha's vision just yet. "Why not just ask the other *party* for a copy of the covenant?"

"The other party is not exactly what I would called trustworthy. They could easily alter the agreement, and we'd be forced to comply with anything they might find amusing to add to it. It was safer to pass the rules of the covenant to each generation by word of mouth. While we're certain about some of the articles that were written, there are other things that we may be doing unnecessarily. We do know that breaking the wrong rules can have dire consequences."

"So we're doing all this stupid stuff because some witch burned the list of rules two hundred years ago?"

Mom nods. "I'm afraid so."

"And does Mrs. Keyes know you're telling me all of this?"

"After Sascha's initiation there was talk, and then after

Dani's unfortunate reaction it was agreed that you and Zahara should be given basic information."

"Well, you can cross riding the sticks home after a kill off the list. Dani and I hitched a ride home one night and we're all still here."

Mom stiffens. "I hope I've made it clear how foolish that was."

"Maybe if you'd told me about this covenant nonsense before, I would have known that!"

"We assumed you were all following the rules!"

"Yeah, 'cause kids are always doing what they're supposed to."

Mom narrows her eyes and I have to wonder if they were really that naive.

"So," I say, "I *assume* the big eighteenth-happy-birthday reveal is the covenant?"

"Yes, there is information that was deemed to be sensitive in nature, and when the agreement was made it was decided it should only be shared when you were old enough to fully"— Mom pauses, appearing to look for just the right word—"to fully comprehend what was being expected of you.

"That's why it was imperative to keep Dani from talking. She was upset and not thinking clearly. Surely you understand she was putting lives at risk."

I get up from the table and take a deep breath. "I understand

Dani knew the risks and she decided I needed to know what was going on anyway. And while I appreciate you throwing me a bone tonight, I'm not placated, pacified, or satisfied to wait until my birthday to find out what the hell is going on. Good night, Mom."

"On July 7, 1991, Sascha's mother refused to go on a hunt," Mom says, and I freeze in my place. "Sascha was two, fussy, and her father begged Mrs. Ramirez to stay home. The rest of us went, completed our hunt successfully, and brought back a powerful talisman. But it didn't matter. In the morning Mr. Ramirez was gone."

"He left them?" I ask, but I already know that's not what happened.

"He was taken," Mom says, "to punish Mrs. Ramirez for defying the covenant. Thank goodness, Sascha was too young to remember, but it happened right in front of her."

I turn to Mom and look her in the eye. "How many other people have been taken by demons?"

I expect to see her look shocked, but she doesn't. She just shakes her head. "How did you know?"

"How many people?"

Mom folds her hands in her lap, takes a deep breath, and exhales slowly. "Fifteen, though only ten people were taken with witnesses present, the other five could have disappeared for a variety of reasons. How did you know?"

"Dani and I activated the birthstone necklaces. Margo and Sascha had a vision or a premonition of a demon in the meetinghouse, and apparently someone's going to Hell."

Mom gasps. "Julia, you see, we have to convince Dani to stay and do whatever needs to be done!"

"Her mind seemed pretty made up."

"Make sure she changes it! What if Mrs. Robbins is taken—or Dani?"

"I would never let that happen!"

Mom relaxes a bit. "Okay, then. You know what you need to do. And while I've never used birthstones before, premonitions are often just a shadow of what *might* come true. They can be prevented from happening."

I think about Mr. Ramirez and get an awful thought. "Did my father get taken?"

Mom shakes her head, and tears well up in her eyes.

"Is he really dead?"

She shakes her head again. I look away, and focus at the witch balls hanging on the curtain rod over the sink. "Where is he?"

Mom doesn't say anything.

"*Where is he?*" I ask again.

"I don't know. After Mr. Ramirez was taken, your father and I decided that as much as he loved us, he couldn't stay. I wiped out his memory with a spell, and he left to start over. I don't know where he is now, but—" Mom's face crumples in tears. "I have a witch ball in my studio that glows when he's happy. He loved you, Julia, but I couldn't let him get taken!"

"So let me recap this," I say, tears welling up in my own eyes. "My father isn't dead. Just memory-impaired. I don't exist in his mind. We're bound by some covenant that we don't know all the rules to, and messing up gets someone dragged off to Hell. Have I got everything?"

Mom doesn't say anything. Her chin quivers as she nods.

"And this is just the good stuff, right? On my birthday you'll be dumping something worse on me. Can't wait."

"I wish it didn't have to be this way," she whispers. "I wish I could have given you a different life."

"You know, Mom—despite everything you've told me, I'm not convinced you couldn't have. Dani may have been overreacting, but I don't think she was. I think she's just braver than everyone else here."

I stalk off toward the stairs.

"Julia, wait." Mom rushes past me and stands at the bottom of the stairs blocking my way. "Don't do anything rash. It won't be long until your birthday—wait until then before you decide to do anything."

I look into her frightened eyes and feel nothing. No fear, no sadness—just emptiness. "I can't make you any promises."

I walk past her and up into my room. I sit on my bed and

stare at the black window. The new purple witch ball Mom made me to replace the one Margo broke sways a bit on its string. "Damn it!" I yell, pointing my hand toward the ball. The ball glows for a second and then shatters. Glass clanks on my floor and bounces on my comforter. I hear Mom pause outside my bedroom, and I pray she won't come in. I exhale as I hear her move down the hall toward her room.

There really isn't anything else to say—is there?

14

I stare at the ghost ball Mom just put in front
of me. It's a light transparent blue. Here I thought she was
spending the last two days in her shop so she could avoid my
sullen looks and silent accusations. Apparently she was just
finding a way to keep the balls blue.

It's hard to imagine I was joking around about blue balls
just a few days ago. Nothing seems very funny anymore.
Everyone is lying low—avoiding everyone else at home and
at school.

I look up at Mom with what I hope is a look of utter dis-
dain. "Congratulations, Mom, you did it. So glad you didn't
let the new ghost ball enterprise fall by the wayside while we're
in the midst of a crisis here."

Mom gives me the same half smile she's been plastering on

her face lately—the "I know things are tragically wrong but I'm going to pretend otherwise" smile. "Life goes on."

"Yeah, wonder how Dad's new life is?"

"Julia!"

"I know," I say holding my hands up in front of me. "Don't start—you didn't have a choice, and no, I wouldn't want my father dragged off to Hell, either."

She gives me the little smile again—though there is a hint of crazed frustration in her eyes. I have to commend her on her ability to keep it cool when I've been baiting her every chance I get.

"But," I continue, "you don't seriously expect me and Dani to go out and test this for you? Dani's barely functioning despite all of your assurances she'd get over *it*, not to mention that she has a chem quiz tomorrow. I'm beginning to think there's some sort of conspiracy afoot."

I raise my eyebrows up and down, and suppress my own smile as I see Mom's get tighter and more forced.

"We've had an awful lot of hunts and such on Tuesday nights—and everyone knows she has a quiz every Wednesday."

"No one is trying to sabotage Dani's GPA. We just think it would be good to get her back out in the hunt and this will be an easy job. It's just one ghost at an old farmhouse."

"Was the deceased burned, butchered, or bludgeoned to

death? It would be totally cool if he or she'd been burned. Then you'd have a trio of barbecued ghosts, and you could sell them as a set!"

"It's not even a poltergeist, just a lingering shade," Mom says, obviously trying very hard to keep her voice calm. "But I hope you know your attitude isn't making things easy here, and it certainly won't help Dani, either."

"I wasn't trying to be helpful."

"Then do it for Connor."

My eyes go wide, and I feel my chest flush. "Wha—why would I want to help Connor?"

Mom looks smug. "We're not idiots, either," she says slowly, her narrowed eyes locking into mine.

"Fine," I say, getting up and taking the ghost ball out of the box. I throw it up in the air and love her worried look as I catch it clumsily. I'm wondering if the only reason Mom isn't coming down on me about Connor is because she's trying to keep me happy so I don't do anything that, in her opinion, would be foolish. "But why can't we leave Dani out of it? I'll go alone, or take Sascha."

Mom shakes her head. "You're Dani's best friend, it'll be good for you two to have a chance to talk. She needs to get out. Despite the difficulties we've been having, helping people is our number one mission and she needs to, as you kids say, get her game face back on."

I scoff. "I'll be sure to tell her that—no doubt they're just the words of wisdom that will finally snap her out of her funk!"

"She'll be here shortly. She and her mother were meeting Helena at the coven house for a little talk," Mom says, ignoring my comment.

I roll my eyes as I reach for my cape. "Why didn't you just have her chat with a snake?" I mutter to myself.

When Dani knocks on the door, Mom rushes over and ushers her in. "We're *so* glad you could help Jules out! This is an easy one—not like the last time. Just in and out and back home."

Dani stares at Mom for a few seconds. "Great," she says without any enthusiasm.

Dani shuffles over to me and I hug her, but she doesn't hug me back.

"I'm on your side," I whisper in her ear. Louder I say, "Let's get some binders and such and some stakes."

"Oh, no need for that," Mom says. "It's just one old farmer who passed away when he was in his nineties."

"Fine!" I say.

I wrap my cloak around my shoulders and sniff the air. A rotten egg–sulfur smell fills the room. I turn and see the cauldron—blue smoke is bellowing out of it. There's so much smoke, the vent above it can't keep up. "What's going on?" I say, coughing.

"You girls head out—I'll take care of it," Mom chokes out. "I put some cleansing herbs into the pot, but maybe they were only meant for outside cauldrons."

Dani and I rush out, coughing, into the cool evening air.

"How are you doing?" I ask when we're both breathing normally.

Dani shrugs. "We fly in darkness—" She pauses as Mom opens a window to let the smoke out. "For the good of all," she deadpans, looking at Mom with utmost loathing. "Let us pass unseen until we land again. "

The mist engulfs us and we fly.

We land in a weedy front lawn after a near silent ride. So much for me being a comfort.

I shine my flashlight on an old farmhouse with a buckling porch, and plywood covering most of the first-floor windows—one board's been pulled down, probably by kids looking for an out-of-the-way place to party. Mom said this was an easy deal, so I'm wondering why the hairs on the back of my neck are standing up.

I turn to Dani. "Well, doesn't this just scream haunted house?" I immediately know that was stupid thing to say. We should be talking about other things, but part of me wants to wait for her to take the lead.

"Tell me about it," she says in a flat voice. She rubs her

hands up and down her arms. "I have goose bumps."

I nod and realize I'm holding my broom in a death grip, and relax my hand. "Something feels off." I pull my necklace out, and let it drop back onto the outside of my cape. I'm relieved the stone is dark. "So far so good, I guess."

Dani takes hers out—the stone is dark as well. "Yeah, no poltergeists tonight."

I walk over to the bottom porch step and listen for any noise coming from inside. The noisy ones are the most trouble, so I'm glad things are quiet. Maybe I'm just tense because of everything that's been happening.

"Are you up for this?" I ask.

Dani reaches out and grabs my arm—pointing up toward the second floor. "Did you see something go by that window?"

"No, did it look like a spook?"

"I'm not sure. It seemed pretty solid. Maybe we should call and see if anyone can come out and help." Dani takes out her phone.

"We can do this," I say, hating that I'm sounding like my mother—trying to coax Dani into this hunt.

"I'm not getting a signal anyway." Dani closes her phone and slips it into her cape.

"Well, let's trap it quick, and get you home."

I start up the steps, but turn back when Dani doesn't

follow. She's staring up at the house, shaking her head.

"I can't do this anymore," Dani whispers.

Tears start running down her cheeks. I walk back down and reach out for her hand.

She pulls away from me. "I can't go out on hunts when I know—" Dani shakes her head and takes a few more steps away from me.

"Dani, is it really as bad as you think? Margo and Sascha haven't said anything lately, they seem all right."

Dani scoffs. "Well, Margo's a soulless bitch, and in case you haven't noticed Sascha's boozing it up more than ever—and if everything is so *freaking* all right, why the hell did my own mother cast a spell on me so I couldn't tell anyone what is really going on?"

"Well, there's the covenant and all, and—I don't know what else, but—"

"That's right! You don't know—but I do, and it makes me sick to my stomach just thinking about what's coming. My mother and Helena, and all the rest of them can make sure I can't tell the whole world what we're all about—but they *can't* make me stay."

"You're leaving? I thought you'd at least wait until I—"

Dani gives me a disappointed look. "I *thought* you'd fight for me, but you're just like everyone else."

"That's not fair! I don't know everything. I—"

"You let them talk you out of fighting. You could've asked Margo or Sascha what was going on."

"They won't say anything!"

"Did you ask?"

"They've made it pretty clear they're not talking!"

She shakes her head. "I'll help you catch this stupid spook, and you can bring it back all trapped in the stupid ball so Helena and your mom and *Connor* can congratulate themselves on their clever new way to screw nightmares. But I'm not coming home with you."

"Where would you even go?"

"I'm not sure and I wasn't going to tell you, but you're my best friend and I was hoping I could trust you. I can trust you, right?"

"Yeah. But Dani, I thought we'd be facing whatever it is together. And Connor—he'll help us."

Dani looks up into the sky and laughs. "Jules, we're not going to change things and I have to tell you I wouldn't place any long-term bets on you and Connor."

"What?"

Dani looks at me like I'm crazy. "Open your eyes. Connor isn't exactly moving heaven and earth for you, is he?"

I clutch the ball in my pocket and resist the urge to throw it at her. "He's trying some stuff—he wants things to change."

"Have you slept with him yet? Have you gotten past doing everything but *it*?"

"God, Dani!"

"You don't need to answer. I know you haven't, and I know why, because Connor's toeing the line. Hell, he probably knows everything."

"What are you talking about? Why are you acting like this?"

"Because I know the truth!" Dani stalks up the porch stairs and raises her hand in front of the door. "Open!" she yells, and the door rips off its hinges and crashes to the floor. She turns to me. "Let's get this freaking thing over with so I can get the hell out of here, and away from all this crap!"

"Dani, come on, talk to me!"

"Just give me the damn ball!" she yells.

I take it out of my pocket and toss it over to her. She barely catches it and rolls her eyes at me. She walks into an empty room to the right of the door and kicks a soda can. "Are you ready?"

"Yes!"

"Good!"

She holds the ball out, and then we stand back-to-back. I face my palms out, and yell, "*Reveal!*"

I look around the room, wondering where the ghost will

manifest, and suddenly a bat flies down from the ceiling, and morphs into a man. He smiles, revealing two sharp canine teeth.

"Vampires!" Dani yells.

I reach into my cape. My heart starts to pound when I remember I don't have a stake or binders.

I turn my head, and see a second vamp in front of Dani. I start to run but the vamp closest to me leaps out, grabs my shoulder, and flips me so my back is pinned to his chest. I try to pull away as I watch Dani, wrapped in the arms of the second vamp, struggle and kick.

"Ladies, so nice of you to come," my vamp says.

"We're not after you—we're looking for a ghost," Dani chokes out. I see Dani's necklace resting on her chest—the charm that would've protected her gone.

Her vamp smiles and I'm glad Dani can't see the hunger that consumes his face as he draws his lips back and sinks his teeth into her.

She lets out a surprised gasp. The ball drops from her hand, rolling across the floor to a corner. I look away and kick my heels into the vampire's legs.

"No worries, sweetheart," he whispers, pulling me closer. He runs a hand up my right side, lingering on my breast, and against my will, all the fight leaves my body. His cool lips run across my jaw up to my ear. "No worries."

"Let me go," I say, but there's no force behind my words. I try to think of a spell to make him release me, but my head is foggy. I close my eyes and concentrate on the icy trail his mouth is leaving on my skin—his hand under my shirt. I don't think I've ever felt anything so wonderful. I lean back into him and tilt my head to the side. Each of his kisses sends an electric shock through my body. My eyes flutter open and I see the other vamp's mouth vigorously moving on Dani's neck.

Oh, God, I want that, too. "Please, please," I whisper. "Do it, please."

"Whatever you want," he says. He reaches a hand under my shirt—lightly running his cold fingers over my bra. My legs buckle and he holds me tighter. Then I feel it. His teeth pierce the thin skin on my neck just below my ear, and I'm in heaven. The room disappears as my blood flows into him. My mouth opens like a fish gasping out of water.

He pulls away from me and nuzzles my neck.

"No, don't stop," I plead.

"Oh, I'd love to have you drink and join us," he whispers. "It would be so easy to finish this, but it's not to be—at least, not tonight." He licks and kisses my neck, and the hunger welling inside me is unbearable. "But I'll put you out of your misery."

He turns my shoulders so I can face him. I tilt my chin

up, and his dark eyes burn into mine. He kisses my cheek and then my mouth. I hungrily kiss him back—tasting my own blood.

I press my hips into him, and he peppers my neck with kisses. He drags the tip of his teeth across my skin and I feel like I'll explode waiting for him to sink the tips into me again.

"Do it, do it," I whisper.

"Whatever you want, love."

I feel the sharp prick and the force of his mouth sucking hungrily on my neck and I never want it to end. "Oh, God, yes," I moan as the room fades to black.

"Jules?"

I feel hands shaking me, but I'm too tired to move.

"There's blood on her neck." I hear someone say.

"Oh, my God, is she—?"

Someone grabs my wrist.

"She's got a pulse."

"Thank God."

"Jules!"

I open my eyes, see Sascha hovering over me, and turn my head away from the liquor burning off her breath. God, I hate brandy! "Leave me alone." My neck hurts, I feel empty and weak.

Fingers grasp my chin, and Zahara gets in my face. "Jules, what happened—where's Dani?"

It comes back to me.

The vamps.

The teeth.

How much I liked it.

I try to push up on my arms to look for Dani but my elbow collapses. "Vampires," I whisper. "Two of them."

"How the hell did you get caught?" Zahara asks.

"We didn't have any binders—it all happened so fast. They just grabbed us and then—"

Zahara looks up at the ceiling and shakes her head. "How could you be so stupid? You never go out without binders!"

"We were just after a ghost. We didn't think—"

"Damn straight, you didn't think!" Zahara says. "You're lucky you still have a pulse!"

Sascha helps me sit up. "Look around for Dani, I'll stay with her."

When Margo and Zahara leave the room, Sascha leans in close to me. "I was afraid something like this would happen," she whispers.

"What?"

"I think they're trying to scare you and Dani."

"The vamps?"

"No—our mothers."

"We were just testing the new ball. My mom thought it would be an easy job; she didn't know vamps were hanging here."

Margo comes down the stairs. "The place is empty—just a couple of dead rats the vamps were snacking on." She looks down at me. "Before the main course arrived."

"That's not funny," Sascha says.

"Well—" Margo pauses like she knows that was a shitty thing to say. She looks away. "It was just a joke," she adds quietly, apparently unable to stop herself from using her usual tagline.

"Dani's *got* to be here. Wait, is her broom out front?" I ask, hoping it's gone and she's just flown off instead of dead.

Z walks in. "Yeah, both of your brooms are leaning on the porch rails, we saw them when we landed. Look, I don't see any sign of her or the vamps. Why don't we head home and get some help. Helena might be able to do some tracing spell. Can you fly?"

My head throbs when I stand up, and I feel weak. "Yeah, I think so."

"Huh," Margo says, walking across the room. She bends over and then holds out the witch ball I'd brought. "Looks like there was a ghost after all."

"No," I say, taking the ball from her hand, but as the words come out of my mouth, I wonder if I'm wrong. A burning, white light is banging around furiously inside the ball, weaving up and down the glass threads, like it's trying to find a way out. "When we revealed I didn't see a ghost, just the two vamps, but maybe one got sucked in while I was—"

"Meat?" Margo asks.

Sascha turns to Margo. "What the hell is your problem? Dani's missing after a freaking vampire attack, and you're dropping one-liners?"

"She didn't mean it," Zahara says. "Right?"

Margo snatches the ball out of my hands. "Yeah, and I don't think anything's happened to Dani. She's been so pissy about everything, she probably needed some time alone to think."

"No," I say. "You didn't see it. I don't think that was something Dani could have walked away from on her own!"

Margo raises her eyebrows. "You seem to have pulled through okay. But since I've never been stupid enough to let a vamp get close enough to bite to me, I'll have to take your word for it."

I stare at her and tell myself to keep control. But I can't. I slap her face with as much force as I can manage and stumble as my knees give out from under me.

Sascha catches me, but I wobble in her arms. "Jules!"

Zahara grabs my other arm and pulls us both up. "Hey! Cut it out!"

"What the fu—" Margo sputters, holding a hand to her face. "My nose is bleeding!"

I wrap one arm around Zahara's neck to steady myself. "Just be happy I'm weak from having my blood drained, because I was trying to break it. But let me be the first to congratulate you on finally becoming the über-bitch you've been in training for. I thought maybe you were on our side, but it's obvious you'd rather be Helena's pet hunter."

Margo walks up to me and pokes my chest with a finger. "You know what, Jules? You'd just better back off, because you don't know the half of it! And don't think Helena is going to let you keep dicking around with Connor if you're not one hundred percent behind the coven! Not that you really have a choice. None of us do!"

We all stare at Margo.

"What?" Zahara asks. She turns to me. "You and Connor are like—together? And Helena knows?"

Margo holds a flashlight under her chin, illuminating her face. "God, Z, I thought Dani was supposed to be the thick one. But yeah, Helena knows, and she's not happy." She flicks the light off and brushes past me. "I'll be at the meeting-house," she calls back to us. "Helena's gonna want to see this ball and hear what happened."

She thunders down the porch steps and I hear her mutter the cloaking spell.

"I can't take this anymore!" Zahara says, her hands curled into fists at her sides. "Sascha, you've got to tell us something!"

Sascha slumps against the wall. She closes her eyes, and Z and I exchange looks, and I wonder if Sascha's passed out.

"Sascha?" I say.

She opens her eyes, takes out the flask, and brings it to her lips again. She throws it back and takes a long swig, and then hands it out to Zahara. "Here, this helps. Some."

Z shakes her head. "I don't want the freaking booze—I want answers!"

"Okay," Sascha says. She stands up and sways a bit. "I've been in hell since my birthday—figuratively—but I've kept it under wraps with a little help." She shakes the flask and lets out a quiet laugh. "Dani, on the other hand, leaves *her* initiation a little nuttier, runs her mouth, and gets a very powerful spell cast on her. She doesn't show signs of improvement, and people are very careful about what they say around her, not knowing what will set her off again."

"Your point?" I ask.

"My point is, I was being the good, quiet witch who fades into the background making it easy to forget I'm there—easy to talk in front of me." She takes another swig. "And I overheard my mom on the phone last night, she said she wasn't sure if 'scaring them straight' was the best tactic, but she'd go along with it if the majority ruled."

"And you think that's what happened?" I ask. "Our mothers set us up?"

Zahara kicks an old beer can across the floor. "With vampires?" she says, rolling her eyes toward the cracked ceiling. "That's crazy!"

"Crazy, yes," Sascha says, "but not the least bit surprising." She takes another drink and puts her arms around Zahara and me. "Our mothers have taken the term 'evil bitch' to a whole 'nother freaking level."

I think about my mom emphasizing the coven mission before we went out tonight. I could almost see her thinking an unexpected attack might make me feel a little more willing to go out and get revenge on the next set of bad guys—make me feel the bloodlust a little more.

My hand reaches up for my necklace. The stone didn't light up despite the fact Dani and I reactivated them just yesterday.

Of course, if there's a spell to activate stones, why not one to deactivate them? I wonder if such a spell might involve a cauldron and herbs that turn the steam into a thick, swampy, blue mess. I shake my head. She couldn't have. She wouldn't have.

"You really think they sent the vamps to rough us up?" I ask.

Sascha nods. "The question is," she says, looking around the empty room, "did one of the vamps take things too far?"

15

I look out my living room window and see the moon hanging orange and low in the darkening sky. It's waxing and should be full within the next few days. It's been just over twenty-four hours since Dani disappeared. I wonder if she can see it wherever she is.

I rub the top of Nuisance's head, and he gives a sleepy trill. *Was Dani really taken by the vamps?* I've asked myself this a million times today, while carefully avoiding thinking too long about the next logical question.

If so, will we have to hunt her down?

I squeeze my eyes tight and hear Dani's voice in my head stating the obvious like she always does. *Well, hunting vamps and werewolves* is *what we do.*

I stare at my cell phone sitting on the coffee table and will myself not to call Connor again. He wasn't any help anyway.

Don't worry, babe, I'm sure she'll turn up. You know how mad she was, she's probably just trying to get her head together. I really can't talk right now—my mom's hovering and something big is going on. Call you later!

What could be bigger than Dani disappearing?

But maybe that's what he meant, and it just didn't come out right.

Mom walks in with her cape on. I keep petting Nuisance, and pretend I don't see her.

She sits next to me and reaches out and kneads her knuckles on top of Nuisance's head. "I have to go out for a little while. We're having a meeting to try to sort out what happened, and figure out what to do next. And to find Dani."

She pauses and I wonder if she realizes that her "find Dani" sounded like an afterthought. I stare down at Nuisance, concentrating on the deep rumblings coming up from his throat.

"I know how hard this is for you," she says. "If I had known what was going to happen, I *never*—"

She takes a deep jagged breath, and I try to think of something snarky to say. I could ask her how the ghost ball biz is going, or if she could've come up with something a little less lethal than a vampire attack to ensure Dani got a zero on the chem quiz—but I decide to play it Sascha's way and keep things cool.

"Yeah, it's hard. Really hard." I look at her and see she isn't wearing the plastered-on smile that's been the norm lately—her face is drawn and blotchy from crying.

I haven't cried yet. I thought if I could hold out and be strong, Dani would come home and we could laugh about the good scare she gave everyone. I think I was worried if I did cry, it'd mean Dani was dead—or worse.

I let Mom wrap me in her arms, and now I can't hold back the tears any longer. She hugs me tight, and I have to believe Sascha got it all wrong. Our mothers couldn't have set us up.

"Mom, I'm so scared. I thought for sure she'd call me today. But she—"

Mom hugs me tighter, and then smoothes my hair with her hands. "I know, sweetie. We're all scared, but we've put the word out on the street to look for her." Mom gets up and blots her eyes on the edge of her cape. "I can stay if you want me to."

"No, that's okay. I want you to find Dani."

"I'll call you if we hear anything."

There's a knock on the kitchen door and my heart skips a beat. "Dani?"

Mom shakes her head. "I'm sure if it was Dani she'd go home first. I'll see who it is."

I'm thinking home is probably the last place Dani would go. I pull the blanket up to my chin and hope if it isn't Dani it's Connor. Surely after everything that's happened he could come over—it's not like we're a secret anymore.

Nuisance jumps off my lap and follows Mom into the kitchen. I hear the kitchen door open.

"Michael, how nice of you to come over."

I sigh.

"I'm just on my way out, but Julia's in the living room. I'm sure she'd love someone to talk to."

I'd *love* to talk to Connor, but I guess Michael will have to do.

The door shuts, and I sit up and run my fingers through my hair. "Hey," I say when he walks in.

"Hey," he says quietly as he takes off his coat and sits next to me. "I just thought you might need some company." He takes my hand, and a tear rolls down my cheek.

"Dani's tough, Jules—tougher than people give her credit for."

I lean into him and breathe the November air clinging to his flannel shirt. "I don't think she's coming home."

He doesn't try to dissuade me, and I'm figuring he's come to the same conclusion.

"And," I continue, "I won't be able to tell her I'm sorry." I take a deep breath and decide to tell him the other thing I've been trying not to think about.

"We got in a fight just before it happened," I whisper. "She didn't think I had her back—and I didn't. She was so upset after her initiation and I didn't try hard enough to help her. And I let the vamp take her. I didn't even try to stop it." I look up into his brown eyes, wondering if he'll be sorry he came over—sorry he tried to comfort someone who let their best friend go down in flames.

"Hey," he says, squeezing my hand. "It wasn't your fault. You guys aren't invulnerable, and from what I've heard, vamps can really mess with your head."

"Oh, yeah." I sigh, remembering how powerless I felt.

He leans away from me and tilts his chin down. "And a lot of weird shit has been happening, that's the other reason I came over." He looks around the room like he's not sure if he should go on. "I heard my mom talking to Mrs. Keyes on my back porch," he says finally.

I wipe my sleeve across my eyes and cheeks. "Were they talking about Dani?"

Michael nods and furrows his brow like he's not sure he can tell me what comes next.

"Michael! What did they say?"

He takes a deep breath. "Mrs. Keyes figured that the vampire who got to Dani wouldn't turn her because then Dani would talk. She figured she'd—"

"Be able to identify him?"

"No," Michael shakes his head. "She figured Dani would

come back and talk to you about what was really going on, and the vamp knew better than to let that happen. She said if Dani *did* get turned, they wouldn't send all of you after her— that they'd take care of her themselves."

Overwhelming anger blows away all of the sadness in me. "They've already written her off! They're not looking to find her, they're plotting damage control."

"Hey, it doesn't mean she did get—you know, turned, but I thought you should know."

"But wait, why would she say the 'vamp knew better than to let that happen'?"

"Yeah, I couldn't figure that out, either—it was like she was talking about someone she knew."

My stomach sinks. *No. No. No. Please don't let my mom be involved. Please let this all be Helena's doing.*

"Did they say anything else?" I say through clenched jaws.

"Not really, but like I said, I thought you should know. We have to watch out for one another because sometimes I get the feeling no one else is." Michael looks up at the ceiling. "Don't tell Connor I told you, okay?"

My chin quivers. "Connor knows?"

"I, uh," Michael sputters. "I, uh, checked with him first, yesterday—you know, since you're together and his mom's involved."

"Why didn't he didn't want me to know?"

"Well, maybe he was just trying to protect you."

I let out a long sigh. "Or maybe he was trying to keep me in the dark."

Michael leans over and props his elbows on his knees and sinks his head into his hands. "Maybe."

"You're not going to be like everyone else, and try to convince me everything's fine?"

Michael shakes his head. "No. I kind of get the feeling Connor has changed, or I don't know what, but he's not the same the guy he was even last week. I don't want you to get hurt."

I want to say Connor's changed because of me, because we're together—but I know that's not true. Something happened after his mother caught him sneaking home after our first night together. And no matter how hard I've tried, I haven't been able to stop all the nagging doubts about him from constantly surfacing in my head.

Michael turns to me. "I've been asking my mom a lot of questions after I gave you and Dani that ride home the other night. I got to thinking, I'm doing all this body disposal and nonsense for the coven, so I should know how things work, right? But my mom got all weird on me, and after I kept bugging her she finally said I needed to mind my own business."

"What?"

Michael nods. "Exactly! Cue the what-the-eff-moment.

She's not bagging bodies, I am, and I think I have the right to know what's going on. So I go talk to Connor—thinking he's my best friend, and who else would know the scoop better than the guy living in the same house as the coven leader? But Connor got all weird about it, too. We used to kid around about being on the cleanup crew, and all of a sudden he gets his back up. He says he has more important things to worry about. And when I told him about what I heard, he blew up and made me swear not to tell you."

I look out the window at the moon, its orange color fading as it rises higher in the sky. I remember the tiny sliver of moon from Margo's birthday and it makes me think I've been sitting around on my ass waiting for someone to reveal the truth—or for things to magically get better. I've been letting the doubts about Connor fester for too long.

It's time I got a little more proactive.

I need to get back into that room and see what Connor and Helena have really been up to. And I need to know if Mom deactivated the stones that could've warned Dani and me about the vampires.

Michael brushes aside his long blond bangs. "Something bad is going down, isn't it?"

"Yeah, I think so. I need to figure out if my mother is involved."

"Do you want some help?" he asks.

"Maybe, but I have to do a little digging on my own first, okay?"

"You sure?"

"Yeah."

Michael nods and gets up. I toss him his coat, and he pulls his arms through the sleeves. "You know you can call me if you need anything."

"I know—thanks." I hug Michael, and when he hugs me back I think how absolutely wonderful it feels to know he's willing to fight. I pull back and wish I had the same feeling about Connor.

"We'll get through this," he says.

Hearing him say it makes me think we might.

I shut the door behind Michael, and go back into the living room to the bookshelves. My eyes trace the bindings over and over again, looking for the red leather spine of the *Birth Signs, Stones, and Spells*. It's a large book—it should be easy to find, but I don't see it. I do notice some books look like they've been moved to disguise a gaping hole.

Please let me be wrong. Please don't let Mom be involved.

I trace each of the spines with my finger one more time as I read each title out loud.

I stare at the shelves and think about where Mom would've put the book. It could be in her room—I rarely go in there— or the shop. She doesn't think I *ever* go in, and she's been spending an awful lot of time there lately.

I run outside and grab the key on the door frame. I open the door and flip on the light switch. Mom's been busy. There are at least two dozen blue ghost balls hanging on a makeshift line she's strung up. I see a bucket of broken brown glass where she tossed the defective ones before she got the spell right.

I duck under the line and walk over to her reference books and immediately see what I'm looking for. My heart sinks as I pull the book down.

"Damn."

I take it over to the couch, prop it up on my knees, and flip to the table of contents. Chapter seven—"Activating Birthstones." I scan the table of contents, but don't see anything about deactivating them and a rush of relief floods through me. I stand up to put the book back, but a voice tells me to keep looking. I sit down again and flip to the index in the back.

"Deactivating birthstones," page 184.

I take a deep breath and turn to page 184. *If one wishes to cease the stone's flashing and pulsing to avoid detection, one can easily disable or deactivate them. To temporarily disable a stone, burn a white candle infused with sage—make sure the stone passes through the smoke to ensure the full effect.*

To permanently disable a stone, sage should be boiled in a pre-

enchanted cauldron with at least two cups of Dead Sea salt. Once the stone is exposed to the blue smoke it becomes permanently closed to re-enchantment.

I slam the book shut and reach for my necklace. I look down at the turquoise stone.

She did it. My mom, who not too long ago hugged me and said she was scared, screwed us over. She disabled the only thing that could have protected Dani from a potential *untimely death.*

I throw the book across the room. "How could you?" I scream. A pulse of light leaves my body. It hits the witch balls hanging on the curtain rod, and then the window overlooking the pond. Glass shatters everywhere and I shield my face with my arm.

"Shit!" I scream. I look out onto the pond, wondering how I'm going to explain smashing the window.

"That'll teach her!" a voice says from outside. I freeze in place as a twig snaps. Dani appears on the other side of the window and waves. "Did ya miss me?"

16

"Oh, my God, Dani!" I run toward the window, but she shakes her head and points toward the door.

I turn and run for the door, my heart swelling with relief as I grab the knob. I open it and burst into tears, seeing her standing in front of me—alive. "You're okay!" I sob.

"Glad to see you, too!" Dani shrugs in the darkened doorway. "Um, aren't you gonna ask me in?"

"God, quit joking around and come in already!" I say, pulling her cape and dragging her in.

I throw my arms around her and then stiffen as Dani's icy cheek touches mine. "No!" I push her away and look around the room, searching for something to defend myself.

Dani takes a step toward me and tips her head to the side. "I'm afraid so. I probably should have told you right away, but my hands are kind of tied when it comes to getting into buildings now, and I didn't think you'd invite me in if you knew."

My heart pounds as I take another step back, glass crunching under my feet. I bump up against the couch and feel the cold breeze pouring through the broken window onto my back. I look at her and notice a slight blue tinge coloring her jaw.

She cocks her head and gives me a strange, vacant look. "Yes, it's true. The little white dove that lived within me, helping me along the path to righteousness, is gone." She throws her shoulders back and smirks. "All that's left is a big black thing roosting inside me, *whispering to me*"—she smiles, revealing two long teeth—"telling me to attack."

She starts to laugh, and my body tenses waiting for Dani to make a move on me. She takes a step, and I turn and jump on the couch and try to scramble out the window. Glass cuts into my left hand, and then Dani grabs the collar of my shirt and yanks me back in, tossing me on the floor like a doll.

"What are you doing?" she asks. "You're gonna hurt yourself."

I look up at her, wondering if I'll be able to walk away from an attack like last time. My stomach twists painfully; I don't want to think about Dani doing that to me.

Dani rolls her eyes. "Stop looking at me like that, Jules, I'm not going to bite you. What I said was from those books!"

I keep watching her, not sure what she's talking about, but ready to move fast if I have to.

"The Vampire Stakes books?" She looks at me expectantly. "My *favorite* series in the whole world that you said you'd read." She looks down at me and shakes her head. She holds out her hand for me and laughs again.

"Books?" I ask.

"Yeah, that's what Daemon said to Simone after he got turned by the thousand-year-old vampire *she* was lusting after." Dani looks at me with wide eyes. "You said you'd read them."

My heart is pounding a mile a minute, pumping loads of adrenaline through my body. "I—uh, never got around to it," I say, numbly thinking, *Dani's a vampire and she's standing over me quoting lines from a book.*

She holds her hand out again, and I study her face. Vampires are experts at the art of deception, but if she wanted to get me she could have done it when she first came in.

I reach out toward her, and shudder as her cold hand clamps down on my wrist. I hope I'm not making a deadly mistake.

She yanks me up easily and I take a step away from her, ready to try the window again if she makes any sudden moves.

"Sorry for slamming you on the floor like that—I'm not

used to all the extra muscle power yet, but you can relax." She holds her hand up like she's taking an oath. "I *swear* I have no intention of biting you 'cause that would be, like, really weird and gross, snacking on your best friend! I would appreciate it if you could wrap something around your hand, though. It's hard to concentrate with you bleeding all over the place."

"Sure," I whisper, not believing the turn in conversation.

I shuffle over to take Mom's apron off a hook by the door, not taking my eyes off Dani. I wrap the apron tightly around my hand, wishing this were a dream.

"Thanks!" Dani smiles.

I see her new teeth again and burst into tears. "I'm so s-sorry my mother helped set us—"

Dani comes over and hugs me like everything is okay and she's just plain old Dani. "Come on—stop," she says. She pulls back and gives me a little smile. "At least our mothers didn't *mean* for me to get turned—they weren't being *totally* evil—well, this time anyway. And the vamp that got carried away and did the deed was really apologetic. So it's all cool."

I stare at her in shock. "How can you be so calm about all this?"

"Being minus a soul changes your perspective," she says, walking over to the couch. "I'm not saying this undead stuff isn't gonna take some getting used to. And I did seriously consider staking the vamp who did this to me, but he's so scared that Helena is gonna sic her minions on him, I took pity. Plus, he's been showing me the ropes—God, what a load of crap we were fed about vampires!"

My eyes widen. "Crap?"

"Yeah. I mean, there are some bad vamps—and sometimes people don't handle the transition well and they go a little bonkers like our very first kill, Miss Melissa, but mostly they just want to survive. Hank—that's the vamp who turned me—he's been telling me where the good places to sleep are, and where to find the people who don't mind sharing a little blood." She winks. "As you know, it really is as good as they say."

My cheeks redden as my hand involuntarily reaches up to the cuts on my neck.

"Anyway, not having a soul has created this peace within me I've never felt before." She smiles and I have to try very hard not to stare at her new teeth.

"I feel free now, and all the things I used to obsess about— my grades, saying the wrong thing, losing fifteen pounds— none of it matters anymore. For the first time I couldn't care less if my thighs rub together when I walk. Do you know how liberating that is?"

I stare at her, dumbfounded.

"I feel like I can finally be me because I no longer give a crap what anyone else thinks."

"But you're—" I can't finish my sentence.

"Dead, yeah." Dani looks out the window and nods. "But on the bright side, I still have my powers, but the spell my mom cast on my birthday went *kapoof* the minute my heart stopped beating. Now I can tell you everything, and we can figure out how to break the freaking twisted covenant our ancestors were stupid enough to sign with a pack of demons."

"Huh?"

Dani looks me in the eye. "You did figure out we were working for demons, right?"

"I thought whoever we signed the agreement with had demons working for them."

"No! *We* are the nonunionized employees of the Revealer Demons from the sixth level of Hell. It's a really sweet deal. The demons gave us the reveal spell to use, which sends the souls of every creature we snuff straight to the Revealer realm. Apparently supernatural souls are a hot commodity down there, and the demons promised to keep the coven coffers stocked, and in the old days keep the pitchfork-wielding nut jobs at bay."

I walk over to the couch and carefully brush some glass aside with my wrapped-up hand. I sit down because I'm starting to shake—but I'm not sure if it's from the cold or from what Dani's just said. "No money is worth working for demons. Why would we do that?"

"Because the demons were smart! Well, depending on which side of the agreement you're on, but they set it up so it was unlikely any witch would try to break it," Dani says. "Five members of the original coven agreed to sign their souls away—"

"What?"

"They agreed to sign off on their souls *until* their daughters are born and get the reveal spell. I won't even get into the ceremony and blood swapping they subjected us to, or the fact that all the other coven members are basically parasites living off the hunters—*but* once the kid has the spell, the mom's soul is free and clear, and the next generation is on the chopping block until they have kids. And so on and so on and so on."

"Oh, come on, no mother would agree to that!"

Dani throws her hands in the air. "But they did—they have! They even use spells to make sure they have girls and get pregnant around the same time. Everyone was acting like I'd lost my mind for being freaked that our mothers knowingly signed off on our souls! I told them not only was there was no way I was gonna do that to my kid, but effective immediately I was off the hunt.

"Of course you have to appreciate the irony seeing as I'm the one without a soul now." She slides her tongue across her sharp teeth. "But you wouldn't believe how many talks with

Helena I had to sit through. It was maddening having her acting all smug, and "we're doing it for the good of mankind" when she doesn't have a lien on her soul!

"Finally I just pretended to give in and said 'I'll hunt, just back the hell off!' I had no intention of keeping my word, though, and that's why I was gonna leave after the ghost.

"But," Dani continues, "I have to imagine the first witches were pretty bad off, way back when—what with people always trying to burn them, and hangings, and such. And maybe they didn't have a lot of food and the winters were harsh—blah, blah, blah, but to keep this going for three hundred years, well, there's no excuse."

I'm thinking losing your soul, or getting personally dragged off to Hell might give a person pause, but I don't want to bring that up since Dani is newly soulless. But soul or no soul, handing your kid over to demons is all kinds of wrong. "So, if I don't have a girl to take the reveal spell and fulfill the covenant, I lose my soul?"

"Yeah," Dani says. "Of course now I feel a little silly about making such a fuss about that part, seeing as it isn't as bad as I thought, but no one has the right to stick it to a kid like that."

I don't even know what to say. Generation after generation of coven woman have traded their own souls for their daughters'. And here I was thinking deactivating our necklaces and sending us to get roughed up by vamps was about as low as you could get.

"I just don't understand how could they do it," I say finally.

"I don't have a clue! But, wait, it gets even better. Hank told me something Helena *et al* didn't share on my birthday." Dani bites her lip, and the tips of her canines hang slightly lower than the rest of her teeth. "Hank and some other folks are on the coven bankroll! We're paying vamps and other werewolves to get names and locations—basically they're snitches. I probably should have staked Hank just for ratting out his own kind, but like I said, he's in so much trouble for turning me that his days are probably numbered anyway. Surreal, huh?"

"Yeah," I say in a whisper.

"Hank said they've even gone so far as to lure people from out of the country to meet quotas."

I look at Dani, sitting across from me on the couch, wishing I could blink my eyes and wake up from this nightmare. The breeze blowing on the back of my head through the broken window is the only thing that convinces me this isn't a dream.

So," Dani continues, "we need to call Margo, Sascha, and Z and tell them I'm okay."

I raise my eyebrows.

"Well, okay enough," she says. "But it's time to figure

out how we're gonna give the coven one long overdue ass kicking!"

"Um." I pause, wondering if everyone is going to accept the new Dani. "That sounds good and all, but you know, maybe I should talk to them first—you know—alone." I shrug. "Just in case."

Dani laughs. "You're right, I could totally see Margo asking questions after she's already staked me. I mean, look what she did to Kelsey."

I hate to admit it, but I think she's painted a fairly accurate picture.

Dani smiles. "There is something I need to do anyway."

My stomach knots up. "You're not going after Helena, are you?"

"Well, she totally deserves a good bloodletting, but if that's what you're worried about—no, I'm not. I don't plan on sinking my new choppers into anyone who doesn't want me to."

"You can't *turn* anyone who wants you to, either!"

"I know! I know! Just because I'm short a soul doesn't mean I don't know the difference between right and wrong." She tilts her head to the side. "I don't think it would bother me if I did do the wrong thing—but still, I know the difference. And really, we've been murdering people since we were thirteen, can you really say offing Helena is any worse than staking some poor vamp?"

"There's a big difference—Helena's human and alive."

Dani raises an eyebrow.

"Sorry—that was insensitive of me, but with you walking and talking right in front of me, it's hard to think of you as dead." I shake my head. "Or undead." I sigh, and don't want to think about all the wolves and vamps we've killed who were probably like Dani.

"Well, you don't need to worry. I'm not planning on confronting anyone—*yet*. I'll be good. I promise." Dani gives me a wide-eyed innocent look.

"Do you still have your cell phone?" I ask.

"Yeah, the battery is getting low, though. I should make a list of things for you to get from my house later—my charger, some clothes, and maybe Mr. Cuddle Bear."

I give her a look.

She cocks her head. "If any vamp makes fun of him, I'll just have to stake 'em."

I shake my head. "Okay, I'll call everyone, and once I make sure everyone is on board, I'll call you and we can figure out our game plan together."

Dani takes my hand in hers and squeezes it tight. Tears well up in my eyes again.

I shake my head. "I really am sorry. I can't believe this is happening."

Dani reaches over and hugs me. I try very hard not to

flinch or pull away as her skin ices mine. "The important thing is we end the covenant," she says. "And if a demon wants to drag me off to hell—so be it. It's not like I have anything left to lose."

Dani stands up and purses her lips. "I'm thinking you're probably not ready to see me turn into a bat yet?"

"Yeah, probably not," I say, wondering how much a person can process in one day.

"It's really totally awesome, though, because when I morph back—I'm *still* dressed!" Dani smiles like that is the coolest thing in the world, and I wonder if I'll ever get used to seeing her with fangs.

I force myself to smile back at her. "Cool."

"Okay," Dani says. "I'll wait for your call, and hopefully I'll have some good news for you, too. Oh, wait. Is my hair okay? I can't see my reflection, which is kind of a bummer."

"I thought you didn't care about stuff like that anymore."

Dani rolls her eyes. "I may not care about my thighs, but I don't want to walk around looking like I'm homeless." She runs a hand through her hair. "So?"

I reach out and brush her bangs to the side. "You're good to go."

"Great!"

She skips out into the night, and I stand in the shop, shaking.

Dani's a vampire.

My father doesn't know me.

My mother sold my soul.

My boyfriend is most likely a lying rat.

I take a deep breath.

I head over to the clothesline holding the ghost balls. I unhook the first one and smash it into a corner of the workshop. The ball bursts apart and I smile despite the tears pouring down my face.

I pick up the next one, and scream as I throw it in another corner. I pick up a third and wing it out the broken window. The ball makes an unsatisfying splash in the pond and I pick up the next one, aim for the front window, and let it fly. It smashes through a bottom pane, and I realize I'll run out of balls long before I'm done crying.

17

Sascha, Z, and Margo are all staring me.

"Well, isn't anyone going to say something?" I ask. I catch a glimpse of myself in the mirror over my dresser and see my eyes are still red and puffy. I glance at the mall photo-booth pictures of Dani and me tucked into the edge of the glass, and realize the overwhelming sadness I'd felt an hour ago has been replaced by a deep desire to make the coven pay for what they did to her—what they did to all of us.

"Well?" I repeat.

Zahara looks down and fiddles with one of the stuffed animals on my bed, and Margo and Sascha exchange looks.

I let out a long exasperated breath. "Dani is not a cold-blooded killer." I pause. "That would actually best describe us, seeing as most of the vamps we've staked were probably just trying to eek out an existence, instead of busying themselves making an army of the undead like our mothers led us to believe."

"You can't *know* that," Margo says finally. "Dani could be lying!"

"Look, Dani could've gotten me any number of times, *but she didn't*. And really, between what you already know about the coven, and what Michael said, does it really seem so out there that our moms lied so we'd happily stake any vamp they sent us after?"

Margo shakes her head. "She's a vampire! And I know she was your best friend, but—"

"I thought we were all friends with her!" I say. "I can't believe you guys are bailing on her like this, and I can't believe you'd think I would put any of you at risk. Are you really going to trust our mothers over Dani?"

Margo puts one hand on her hip. "Even if any of this is remotely true, I don't believe for one second my mom is in on it. She would have told me!"

"Oh, yeah," I say, "like she told you she swapped your soul for hers *when you were still in diapers?*"

"She told me when the time was right, because she didn't have a choice!" Margo yells. "And it's all worked out! No one's lost their soul for three hundred years!"

"Except Dani," Zahara snaps. She looks around at us

with tears in her eyes. "Our mothers could have stopped this. They could have sacrificed their souls so we'd be safe."

"And Dani would still be alive," I add.

"Are you going to sacrifice your soul, Z?" Margo asks. "Are you going to break the cycle?"

Zahara lowers her head again. "I don't know. What does the ceremony involve?" she says quietly like she's not sure she really wants to know. "The one with the demons?"

"Dani didn't say much about that," I say. "Maybe she figured she'd dumped enough on me."

Sascha looks at Margo, who scowls and shakes her head. Margo starts picking lint balls off my flannel sheets.

"Okay," Sascha says. "I really don't think telling you is going to get anyone carted off to Hell." She shakes her long hair out around her shoulders and sighs. "When a hunter's daughter is one year old, a demon is summoned from the Revealer Realm. Instead of the traditional 'cake and ice-cream party,' the mother makes a cut on the baby's foot with a cer-emonial knife. They fill a cup with the baby's blood, and the demon drinks it. Then the demon makes a cut on its hand, and they gather it in a smaller cup and—"

"Oh, no," I say.

Sascha nods. "Yeah, they give it to the baby. The blood exchange passes on the reveal spell and binds the child into the covenant."

Z and I exchange wide, horrified looks.

Sascha gets up and grabs her cape from my desk chair. "Apparently there's a spell so the baby doesn't feel anything." She reaches in the pocket and pulls out the flask, and slaps it into my hand. "Welcome to my nightmare."

I give the flask back to her. "You know, Sascha, I think we need to be as sharp as possible right now." I look her in the eyes. "All of us."

Sascha nods and puts the flask on my nightstand.

"So we need to figure out what we're going to do," I say. "We need to figure out how we're going to break the covenant."

Margo pinches her lips together and squints her eyes. "If we do anything, someone could get taken!" She looks directly at me. "*I'm* not willing to risk my family—we just have to go along and do what we're supposed to. And," she sniffs, "my mother may have gone through that ceremony—because there really *isn't* any choice—but I'm not buying into that nonsense about paying vamps and wolves to work for us!"

"Look, I think we should do some digging in that room at Connor's house," I say. "There's a ledger documenting kills, and a bunch of other notebooks and papers I didn't have a chance to look at. Some of it's got to contain records." I look at Margo. "Maybe records of other employees."

"Oh, right," Margo says. "You think we're just gonna waltz over there and Helena is going to let us have at it?"

I sigh. "Hopefully, Helena is still meeting with our mothers, but you know, I'm not sure Connor will let us in."

"We could cloak ourselves," Sascha says, looking at me sympathetically.

"Yes!" I say. "And we can have Michael take us. He can distract Connor while we sneak in and go to the room."

"Good idea," Z says.

Margo stares at Zahara like she's betraying her. "You don't seriously think we'll find anything, do you?"

"I'd love more than anything if we didn't," Z says.

"Are you with us?" I ask Margo.

"Fine, but I'm not expecting to find anything."

I pick up my cell phone to call Michael and jump when it rings. I frown, not recognizing the number. I click on the phone. "Hello?"

"Hey, Jules. It's Finn."

"Finn?" I shrug in return to the looks I'm getting from everyone.

"How ya doing?"

"I've been better," I say.

"So anything good going on at your house?" he asks.

"Um, no."

"Well, Evan and I are having kind of an interesting evening. Dani's here, and as we haven't seen her in a few days we missed the big fang makeover. While *I* don't necessarily have a problem with it, Evan is a little freaked, and we'd appreciate it if you could come over and get her before he runs into some serious incontinence issues."

"Oh, crap," I say softly. I should've known she wanted to talk to Evan. "Look, don't invite her in. She won't attack you or anything"—I glare at Margo—"but I'll be right over."

"Thanks, Jules," he says. "Oh, wait—hold on. Yes, I *called* her," he says in a muffled voice. "Well, you wouldn't leave. *You* gave Evan her number last week. Actually there *is* a big difference between witches and vampires!"

"Finn, put her on, okay?" I say loudly.

"Huh?" he asks, obviously putting the phone back up to his ear.

"Put Dani on—just open the door and hand her the phone."

"What are you doing? No, no! Don't open it," Evan calls out in a high-pitched squeak.

"For the hundreth time, stop being such a wuss—she can't come in unless you invite her," I hear him say to Evan. "She wants to talk to you," he says.

"Hi, Jules. You don't need to come get me. I was just leaving," Dani says in a pissy voice.

"You shouldn't have gone over there in the first place! Given what you know about Evan, didn't you think he might be a bit freaked out that you're a vampire?"

"Well, *I kind of hoped my boyfriend would've been a bit more understanding!*" she shouts.

"You were gonna put the vamp spell on him, weren't you?"

Dani sighs. "Okay, fine, maybe I was," she says so quietly I can hardly hear her. "I wasn't gonna bite him, though. I was just hoping using the vamp mojo would *finally* get a rise out of him.

"But I guess it's okay to tell him I always had a better time with Finn anyway!" she says more loudly. "Oh, Jules, Finn is a werewolf."

"Give me the phone!" Finn yells in the background.

I hear some scuffling with the phone.

"I am not!" he says.

I roll my eyes. "Yeah, you know what, Finn? With the day I've been having, you could tell me you're a brain-sucking zombie, and I wouldn't blink an eye. Just tell Dani to meet us at the park down the street from Connor's house."

I end the call and stand up, ignoring the slack-jawed expression on all of their faces. "Dani was pestering Evan, they were kind of going out, but apparently being a vampire is some sort of deal-breaker. She's going to meet us by Connor's, though. So," I say with a clap of my hands, "I'm ready to check out Helena's secret room—anyone who promises not to stake Dani can join me."

They all still look too dumbstruck for an immediate

response, so I dial Michael's number. "Hey, it's Jules, we're all here at my house, and we're hoping we can make use of your excellent decoy abilities."

"Yeah, sure, what do you want me to do?"

"We're gonna channel our inner Nancy Drew and get to the bottom of some things. We need to sneak into this room at Connor's but we need you to distract him."

"I'll try. When do you want me to come over?"

"Now, but don't come here—meet us by the playground near Connor's."

"I'm on my way."

"Thanks!" I click off my phone. "Let's go!" I head for my bedroom door, and then turn back to them. "Do you think Finn Dolan could be a werewolf?" I ask.

Zahara scoffs. "I don't know what the hell to think anymore."

"*I* could totally see him being a wolf!" Sascha says. "He's always sniffing."

Margo cocks her head. "He *is* always sniffing, isn't he?"

I nod and turn back toward the door. "That would explain a lot."

"Hey," Sascha adds. "I noticed when I landed that your mom's workshop has seen better days—what happened?"

I pick up my broom and walk outside. "I had a little pity party, but I'm over it now."

＊ ＊ ＊

We sit facing out in different directions on the small merry-go-round near the center of the playground, holding binders in our hands—a concession I made so Margo didn't have to worry about Dani sneaking up on us.

"She's probably not gonna show," Margo says. "If she's smart she won't," she adds.

"Would you just relax? Things are tense enough," I say.

"Look!" Zahara says, pointing toward the swing sets.

Dani gives a little wave. "Are we cool?" she asks.

Sascha bursts into tears and looks at me.

"It's OK," I say.

She nods, and goes running over to Dani, hugging her tightly. She takes Dani's hand and leads her back to us.

I look over at Margo and see tears brimming in her eyes.

"We're cool," I say.

We tumble into a big group hug, and then Sascha pulls back.

"Let's see them," she says.

Dani smiles and reveals her new teeth. Margo draws back slightly and Zahara swats her in the arm.

"We're going to Connor's to see if we can find anything that'll help us get out of the covenant with our souls intact," I say. "Michael's gonna distract him and we'll sneak in."

"Someone has to invite me in," Dani says, looking slightly embarrassed.

Margo reaches out and squeezes her hand. "I'll do it."

I smile, thinking there's hope for Margo after all. "Great! We need to go through everything fast so we can get out before Helena gets home. Don't touch any of the stuff lying around—some of it is lethal."

We see the van pull up into the parking lot. "Are we ready?" I ask.

"Oh, yeah!" Zahara says. She puts a hand out in front of her and then we all place one on top.

Dani's cold hand on top of mine sends shivers up my arm. "Let's do it!"

"Can you still cloak yourself now that you're—you know?" I ask Dani.

"Yeah. The other vamps were so jealous. Well, sort of. They can turn into mist, but that's not as cool as being able to become completely invisible. If I were, like, evil I could so sneak up on my victims and they wouldn't know what hit them!"

She notices we're staring at her. "Not that I *would* sneak up on anyone, I'm just saying!"

I shake my head. "Let's fill Michael in, and then knock this coven on its ass!"

18

We wait, cloaked, by the side of Connor's house, and watch Michael ring the bell. After a couple of minutes pass, Connor opens the front door.

"Hey," Michael says. "I was wondering if we could talk?"

Connor hesitates. "I'm kind of in the middle of something."

Michael glances toward where we said would be, and I wish he could see us. I will him not to give up. "Um, I won't stay long, okay?"

Connor looks at his watch. "Yeah, I guess."

I tilt my head toward the rear of the house, and we all slink around to the back porch. I slowly turn the handle and give them the thumbs-up when it moves. I pull the door open just enough for us to slip inside.

As I walk into the dark kitchen I hear Margo whisper, "I invite you in."

"Thanks," Dani whispers back.

We walk past the living room. I look in and see Connor sitting on the couch.

"Yeah, I'm sorry about all that," he says to Michael. "It's just been really tough lately, what with Dani missing. I didn't want Jules to get more upset than she probably already is. And I talked to my mom about it—she was just talking hypothetically about Dani. So it's no big deal."

Dani swats my arm. I turn to her and she rolls her eyes.

We head up the stairs and I cringe with each squeak the old stairs make. I hear Michael talking in a loud voice and know he's trying to cover the noise.

I breathe a sigh of relief when we make it to the room. "The lights are on, Connor must have been up here. *Reveal*," I whisper.

"Whoa," Zahara says quietly. "Look at all of this!"

"Holy shit!" Sascha says.

"Over there." I point to the computer and the desks, and we head toward them. The screen displays Connor and Helena's e-mail. "Look through all the papers and notebooks."

Z starts rifling through some papers while Sascha opens a thick accordion file stuffed full.

"Margo, why don't you look through the file cabinet? Dani,

you could read some e-mails. I'll look through the ledger."

Everyone nods. I turn to look at the three ghost balls lying on the desk in open containers filled with packing material. I shudder as burnt eyes and body parts come in and out of focus in the midst of the green light inside two of the balls. The bright white light in the third ball zips and twists around the glass threads inside and I wonder if it's a different kind of ghost.

"There's just receipts and junk in here," Sascha says. She closes up the file and grabs a notebook.

I start to open the ledger when I notice the box where Connor put the Ouroboros ring is still sitting on the desk. I lift the lid off and unfold the paper lying on top of it.

Dani peeks over from the computer chair and looks in the box. "There's your friend!"

"Yeah, right. Hey, why don't you look through the ledger? It has a list of kills and stuff." I slide it in front of her and start reading the description of the ring. My stomach twists when I get to the third paragraph. *The ring has the unique ability to convince the wearer that the giver of the ring is being truthful— deservedly or not. The Ouroboros's ruby eyes light up in response to the giver's words, and the spell infused with the ring influences the wearer to trust the giver implicitly.*

I resist the urge to tear the paper into a million little pieces. I fold it back up, numbly place it on top of the ring, and replace the lid with a shaking hand. I purse my lips and try to hold back the tears brimming in my eyes. He freaking lied to me and I bought it! Every time I had doubts, I let him drive them away with a kiss.

"There's, like, thousands of kills listed in here," Dani says to me.

"What?" I ask, pretending not to hear her so I can buy myself a few seconds to shake off the crawling feeling I have all over. I wipe my eyes and sniff. I need to focus on why we're here, because given everything going on, my *son of a bitch* boyfriend is the least of my problems.

"*I said* there's thousands of kills listed, and this one nut job who was keeping track in the early 1800s wrote down stuff like they killed a wolf with a mole sprouting three hairs or that some vamp had freckles." She flips the pages toward the back. "And we sure are hunting a heck of a lot more since we took over the job."

Dani runs her finger down a page counting under her breath. "Look at the totals after we started hunting. Ten here in March." She turns the page. "April has, um, twelve. And look at this." She points to the brown writing under the comments about the kills. "*We appreciate your added efforts and will adjust the payment accordingly.*"

"Gotta love a book that lets you converse with demons," I say.

Margo shuts a drawer in the file cabinet. "Nothing out

of the ordinary," she says, giving me an "I told you so" look. "There's just a lot of boring paperwork and Connor's old report cards! You're not dating the sharpest stake in the box, Jules."

I shake my head. He was smart enough to fool me. "Just keep looking."

Dani flips the pages back toward the beginning. "Anyway, if you look at most of the other years, the coven only averaged five or six hunts a month *tops*. A lot of months only have one or two."

"Maybe there's just more nightmares to hunt now," I suggest.

Dani glares at me.

My cheeks flush. "Sorry, let me try that again. Maybe there are more *supernaturally afflicted* humans to *go after*."

"Yeah, but it seems like the increased hunts happened once we took over," she says.

"Holy shit!" Sascha says. "Look at this."

We gather around a large black notebook she's opened. "Maybe this has something to do with the increase in hunts!" She points to what looks like a contract of some sort. "We got paid to stake Kelsey!"

"We know that," I say. "The demons pay us every time we stake someone."

"No, look!" Sascha jabs her finger at the paper. "We got

paid to stake *Kelsey*—like a hit—as in someone paid the coven so we would get her specifically."

"No," Margo whispers.

I scan the page rapidly and stop at the signatures at the bottom. Oh, no.

"Margo," Zahara says, "your mother was the *coven representative* for this—she signed it!"

I point to the other name. "And it looks like Troy Dillon's parents paid the coven five thousand dollars to dust her."

Dani laughs. "So, not only did our mothers sign away our souls, they went and pimped us out as supernatural hit men!"

"Dani!" I say.

"Sorry, hit *people*?"

"That's not funny!" I say through clenched teeth, trying to keep my voice quiet.

Dani gives us all an indignant look. "Why does Margo get to be the only one who can let loose with inappropriate jokes?"

I tilt my head at Margo, whose bottom lip is quivering. Dani rolls her eyes.

"Sorry, that was very insensitive of me," she deadpans. "I need to remember that those of you with souls might get upset about the fact that our mothers are running a coven-based mafia."

"Dani!" I say again.

Margo shakes her head. Her face is pale, and I can see her eyes moving across the page reading the contract. She reaches out a hand and runs it along her mother's signature.

"Sorry," Dani says. She looks at me and mouths, *It was just a joke.*

I turn the page. "This is the wolf we got—the one who was at that bar by the stream—signed by Helena." I turn another page. "Here's the man we got in the mall parking lot. The coven got *thirty thousand dollars* for him; brokered by *my* mother." I look up at the ceiling and shake my head. "Damn it!"

I turn to another page. "One thousand for a vamp." I flip to the middle of the notebook and start reading. "Six thousand dollars for one Jenna Maloney." I look farther down the page. "Seems this woman turned a guy into a wolf, and his parents were willing to pay fifteen thousand dollars to have someone—us—shoot her with a silver bullet. I guess they didn't realize we'd have done it for less."

I rapidly turn the pages and check the signatures. "Looks like all of our moms are in on this."

"What are we going to do?" Margo asks. "We can't hunt anymore—we just can't. But if we don't—that vision."

I put an arm around Margo's shoulders. "What if we summon the demons—maybe we can work something out."

"Oh, man," Zahara says. "That's asking for trouble."

"But I don't understand. *Why* would they do it?" Margo asks, her face red and tear-streaked. "We don't need the money—the freaking demons were taking care of that!"

Sascha puts a finger to her lip and takes a deep breath. "We don't need the money, but Connor *is* trying to sell stuff from past hunts, and there's the new deal with the ghost balls. I wonder if this is more about greed than need. Or maybe our mothers—and Connor—wanted to feel more empowered, to do something for themselves that isn't tied into the covenant."

"If someone was really looking to empower themselves," I say, "you'd think they might have come up with something a little more PC, like maybe getting a job helping the elderly instead of turning their daughters into contract killers."

Dani raises her right hand. "Well, I for one am willing to get dragged off to hell to stop this. I'll sacrifice whatever is left of me to break the covenant and show our moms we're better and stronger than they are!"

"You don't know who they'd take!" Margo hisses. "They probably don't even want *you* since your soul is already floating around!" Her face crumples. "I'm scared. I know my mother did all this awful stuff, but I don't want her taken, either."

Zahara nods.

No one says anything.

"Who here thinks it's not okay to swap demon blood with their toddlers?" Dani asks. "Who thinks our mothers did have a choice, and it was beyond wrong to sign off on their kids' souls? And who the hell thinks this whole coven is way more screwed up than the creatures we've been hunting?"

Margo raises her hand. "I do," she says softly.

The rest of us raise our hands.

"And who says anyone has to get taken?" I ask. "We've killed more than a few demons before."

Dani nods. "We need to tell the stupid coven the gravy train days are over, we're done with the hunt, and if they haven't invested their money wisely, they can get a job bagging groceries or flipping burgers. And if a demon does show up, we kick its ass!"

"We're talking about a whole realm of demons!" Margo says. "Even if we manage to kill one, what's to stop them from sending more?"

"Nothing is stopping them," I say. My heart is racing, wondering if we can go through with this and somehow prevent the vision from coming true. "All we can do is try. Let's go over to the meetinghouse and see if our moms are still there. We can tell them it's over, and then if some demon pops up, we won't be taken by surprise."

I glance at Sascha and hope she's not thinking about her father.

The front door slams and we all jump. "Connor!"

Sascha shuts the notebook and pushes it back where it was.

Footsteps sound on the stairs. We all back away from the desks. "He'll hear us if we try to sneak out," I whisper.

"So what if he does?" Dani says. "We can just uncloak and tell him his mom's a bitch, and then we'll be on our way."

"I—I don't want to talk to him, okay?" I say as the sick feeling in my stomach returns. I really don't think I can face him yet. "Let's just wait and see what he does. Maybe he won't be in here long."

Sascha, Margo, and Zahara nod.

"Whatever," Dani says.

I hear Connor in the hallway and put my finger up to my lips. "Shh."

When he stands in the doorway, he looks around the room with a puzzled expression on his face. I realize the room should have been disguised again. He purses his lips, and then walks over to the desk. He sits and jiggles the mouse. The screen saver disappears and he clicks on an e-mail.

"Oh, my God!" he says.

He takes out his cell phone, and punches a couple of buttons. He taps his foot on the floor and then sits up straight in the chair. "Mom! I just got an update. You were right—the bidding is going crazy now." He nods. "Well, I *know* you're busy, but I thought you'd want to know the ghost balls are in the *five-figure* range. And Mom, get this—Dani's soul is close to a *million*! With forty-five minutes left for bidding,

I wouldn't be surprised if we get double that. Mom, we're gonna be rolling in it!"

"Oh, my God!" I gasp.

Connor drops the phone in his lap, and spins around in the computer chair. I uncloak, and Connor's face pales as his jaw drops open.

"Hang up," I say quietly as everyone else uncloaks, too.

He fumbles with the phone and puts it on the desk. "Jules, what are you do—" He sees Dani and moans. "No."

I stare at him, blood pulsing in my ears. I narrow my eyes and lunge at him. I push him on the chest, and the computer chair slides back and crashes into the desk. "*You bastard*! It's in the other ghost ball, isn't it? Dani's soul is in the other ball and you're auctioning it off!"

I pick up the ball from the box on the desk and hold it up. Dani reaches out for it, and the second I place it in her hand the white light slows and hovers in the center between the two glass threads.

Dani turns to Connor and bares her fangs. "Your auction is officially canceled, asshole."

Connor stares at Dani and shakes his head. "I—I can't. The people running it—"

"Uh," Dani says, "I think it's safe to say that none of us give a crap about the people running it." She slips the ball into her cape pocket. "This belongs to me."

"And you know what?" I pick up one of the ghost balls. "I always thought capturing ghosts was a screwed-up idea, so I'm canceling *this* auction, too!"

Connor jumps up, fear flashing in his eyes. "Jules, I'm so sorry, I didn't want you—"

"We bind you to the earth!" Margo yells. She smacks a binder at his feet and the rug fibers, carpet pad, and carpet tacks form long tendrils that twist and crawl up his legs, holding him in place.

"Let's see, you didn't want me to find out you were a lying shit? Or you didn't want me to find out the way the ring really works? Or you didn't want me to find out you were auctioning off my best friend's soul?"

Connor stammers and holds his hands out. "L-look, Jules, I only used the ring because there were some things I couldn't tell you. I wanted to, but when my mom told me about the covenant with the demons I panicked."

"Then why use the stupid ring at all?"

"Because I knew I'd screwed up, and I didn't want to lose you. I was trying to protect you."

I shake my head. "Even if you're telling the truth now, selling Dani's soul—well, there's nothing more to say, is there?" I toss the ghost ball to Sascha who nearly drops it.

"Jules, let me explain," Connor pleads, his eyes flashing back and forth between the ball in Sascha's hands and me.

"This should be good!" Dani says.

Sascha scoffs and tosses the ball to Zahara who catches it easily. "Yeah, you just try and explain why you thought it was okay to auction off Dani's soul."

"No one knew Dani's soul was gonna get trapped," Connor says, looking around at each of us. "The whole thing was an accident, and it's not like we can put it back!"

"You don't know that!" Z yells.

Connor's worried eyes follow the ball as Z tosses it to Margo. "Well, it's not like breaking the ball would help, it would just release it because she's—"

"Undead," Dani says. "And the vamp that turned me told me all about the scare-them-straight idea *your* mother came up with."

"There could be some spell," I say, "but even if it isn't possible to restore her soul, it is freaking unconscionable that you would even consider selling it!"

"Jules, I didn't want you to know. I'm so sorry," he says. "I *know* it was stupid, I just got carried away. I love you. I was doing this so I could be something more *for you*."

I look into his eyes and think how much has happened since that night I first kissed him—and how now, when I look at him all I feel is empty. I shake my head. "I never needed more," I say quietly. "You really are your mother's son."

"No, Jules, don't say that," he says. "I screwed up, but I'm not like her!"

I turn to Margo and point toward the ceiling. She tosses the ghost ball up, and as it arcs up near the ceiling, I raise my hand toward it.

"Jules, don't!" Connor yells.

"*Open!*" A white pulse of energy leaves me and smashes the ball. Glass tumbles down on Connor as the poltergeist circles the room knocking things from the tables before it zips down the hallway.

I hear doors slamming shut and a loud crash from downstairs. "Gee, I think your house may be haunted, Connor."

I pick up the other ghost ball. "I think we should let this one loose in the meetinghouse." I put it in the pocket of my cape, and ignore Connor's pleas to stay and talk. "You know, we should probably be prepared in case we do run into a demon." I walk over to the table with the swords. The one in the middle quivers as I approach.

"Connor, what's the deal with these?" I ask. "Do any of them cut off the heads of the person picking them up or anything like that?"

"I'm not saying anything until you get rid of this binding crap and agree to talk to me!"

I turn to him with my hands on my hips and I roll my eyes. "Oh, my God! After the stunt you pulled with Dani's soul, you're lucky you're still breathing! So unless you want your nuts zapped, start talking!"

Dani giggles. "Oh, let me do it!"

"I'll help," adds Sascha.

"Me, too!" Z says.

"Okay! Okay!" Connor says in a high-pitched voice before Margo can chime in. He places a hand over his crotch. "Only the one in the middle is enchanted—it works on its own, like whoever is holding it doesn't really have to know how to wield a sword. It anticipates the correct move. Everything else is just a sword."

"I'll take that one," Dani says. "I may be stronger, but I don't know if becoming a vampire has improved my coordination much."

Dani takes the sword and points it in Connor's direction. He flinches when she swishes it around in the air. "You *should* be scared!" she tells him.

I take a sword with a long, curved blade. I hold it up to the light and examine the sharp edge.

"Oh, I like this one," Margo says, taking a double-bladed ax with a jewel-encrusted hilt. "It's pretty."

"Yeah, it's important to have pretty accessories when you're fighting a demon," Dani whispers to me.

I glare at her, and she rolls her eyes.

"This is mine!" Sascha says, taking one with some sort of

long black animal hair hanging from the sword's strap.

Z walks over and takes the sword closest to her. "Let's just get this done and hope we're still walking the earth when we're finished."

I take a deep breath and run a hand through my curls. "Are we ready, ladies?" I ask.

"Hey! What about me? Aren't you at least gonna get the binder off me?" Connor asks.

I walk up to him and look down at his legs. "Funny thing about binders. Usually they just crumble after we kill whomever we had trapped. How badly do you want them off?"

Connor's eyes widen. I can see sweat stains under his arms. "Jules!"

"Don't worry—unless I'm in a kill-or-be-killed situation, I don't plan on hurting anyone ever again. Oh, and by the way, in case you hadn't figured it out—I'm dumping you."

Connor sighs. "Fine! Whatever! But you don't really think they'll just sit back and let you quit? And when my mom finds out the auctions got messed up, she's gonna go ballistic!"

"He's right—demons aren't the only thing we have to worry about," Zahara says. "Even if we bind our moms they could start throwing spells our way."

The ghost in my pocket lets out a long, mournful moan.

"Too bad we couldn't trap their powers in one of the balls," Margo says.

"Maybe we could," Dani says. "We could concentrate on their powers and try a command spell—like *remove* or something. And your mom has a ton of balls in her shop."

I groan. "Not anymore, she doesn't. I kind of pitched a fit after you left and broke them. Wait—I threw one in the pond. We could retrieve it."

Z shakes her head. "One's not enough."

"What if we use it together?" Sascha asks. "If all of us are touching it, maybe it'll work."

"Are you insane?" Connor says. "You can't steal powers!"

"Watch us!" I say. "Actually, that's a good idea. You can come and watch us take down the coven. Something you said you'd help me do until you turned into a greedy, spineless, chickenshit!"

I look at the binder threads wrapped around his legs. "Maybe we can cut them off or try a release spell?"

"I'll try," Dani says, pointing her sword at his legs.

"Oh, no!" Connor says. "I'm staying here. Good luck with your little battle."

"Just shut up already," I say, pointing my hand at his head while I examine his bindings.

I look up and see Connor's mouth clamped shut, and I'm glad I wasn't concentrating hard enough to cause it to be threaded shut like the wolf's mouth. I look down at the bindings. "A release command will probably get them off, don't you think?"

Z nods.

"Dani, can you put the vampire mojo thing on Connor before we try to get these off?" I ask. "If it works then you can walk him over to the meetinghouse with you."

Dani sticks out her tongue. "Only if I have to!"

"Umph!" Connor protests, shaking his head wildly.

Dani looks up at Connor dreamily and runs her fingers along his arm. "Do you want to take a walk with me, asshole?"

Connor's body visibly relaxes and his eyes soften. He nods his head. "Umm."

"That is one badass power!" Z says. She points her hand to Connor's legs. "*Release!*"

The binding slips away from Connor, who is still staring at Dani with a glazed, longing look.

"OK, I'll fly back to my house and see if that ball is in one piece. And I'll see you at the coven house in a few!"

I look around at everyone's faces and wonder if I look as scared and worried as they do. "We can do this," I say, but I'm wondering if this moment marks a new beginning or the end.

19

We stand by a window of the meetinghouse, listening to the argument inside.

"You don't appear to be listening to me, so I'll say it again," Mrs. Robbins yells. "*I don't care if she's been turned*, and you know perfectly well she *can* come home."

"Judy," Helena says calmly, "*you* know perfectly well they could've told her about the contracts. We can't have the girls learning about that yet—it's too soon."

"We wouldn't even be having this conversation if you hadn't come up with the asinine idea in the first place!" Dani's mom lets out a choked sob. "Sending vampires after the girls—I can't believe I let you bully me into going along with that."

"Look," Mom says. "We can't undo what happened, but surely we don't need to make Dani pay for our poor judgment *twice.* If it were Connor we were talking about, you might take a different view on this, Helena."

I look at Dani whose eyes are wide with surprise.

"They're fighting for you!" I say.

She jabs her free hand in the air. "Go moms," she whispers.

Connor leans into her and sighs longingly. Dani nudges him away and sticks out her tongue. "His hand is all sweaty, and he's, like, panting all over me."

"Seeing as Connor is aware of all of our dealings and is not a security risk," Helena says, "I certainly *would* take a different view."

"Associating with low-life vampires," Mrs. Robbins says. "Hiring wolves to spy on each other. Anything to make a buck, and my Dani paid the price!"

"Oh, you all protest now, but you've been perfectly happy living comfortably off the money we've taken in."

"We were perfectly happy before!" Zahara's mother says. "Did we really need to buy all that land and build a meetinghouse?"

"Did we really need better cars?" Margo's mom says.

"It's bad enough we're living under the damn covenant," Sascha's mom says, "and then you browbeat and threaten us to go along with your plans to use the girls as hired guns. We've had enough!"

251

"*I say when it's enough!*" Helena booms. "The demons chose *me* as this coven's leader, and as such I have supreme authority over what activities the coven participates in. Are you ready to follow your husband into hell, Rebecca? Just say the word and I'll summon a demon for you, and Sascha will be an orphan! Or maybe they'll take you, Judy? Is a dead daughter worth an eternity in the bowels of Hell?"

"Yes!" Mrs. Robbins shrieks. "Yes, she is! I am willing to risk anything to get Dani back."

"*So be it!*" Helena yells.

"Uh, guys," I say, "I think it's time we head in there with a new game plan."

I look each of them in they eye and they nod.

"Okay!" I say. "It's time we strip the bitch of her powers and find us a new coven leader!" I take the ghost ball out of my pocket and we race up the steps.

"*Open!*" we yell.

The door slams open and Helena is standing in the middle of the room—her eyes transfixed on a small purple light, the size of an egg, hovering in front of her. "*I summon thee from the place you dwell to come forth and exact my wrath!*"

As the purple light twirls and expands, a foul-smelling wind whips around the room. *This is what brimstone smells like*, I think numbly.

"Hi, Mom," Connor says dreamily. "Why'd ya open a portal?"

Helena jerks her head in our direction. She narrows her eyes and gives us her snakiest smile. "How nice of you to joins us, girls. You're just in time to witness firsthand what happens to bad witches."

"Dani!" Mrs. Robbins yells, running to her.

"Just a sec, Mom," Dani says, holding out her hand like a cop. "We've got some bony ass to kick!"

I hold the ghost ball toward Helena. Margo, Sascha, Zahara, and Dani place their fingertips on it, and we hold our free hands out toward her. "*Remove!*" I yell with the others, hoping we've chosen the right word—hoping we can really steal someone's power.

A blast of white light shoots from our hands and streaks across the room, knocking Helena off her feet. "No!" she screams. Helena sits up, her eyes wide, and clutches her chest as a misty, black steam starts to rise around her. "What—what did you do? Connor! Stop them!"

Oh, shit! I look and realize Dani isn't touching Connor anymore, and he's heading my way with his hand held out and his eyes locked on the glass ball.

"Jules, you don't have to do this. Just give me the ball. There has to be another way," he says. "We can talk with my mom—we can work this out!"

"Just take the damn ball, Connor!" Helena screams.

"I don't think so!" Mom calls out, throwing a binder at him. "I bind you to the earth!" As the binder wraps up Connor's legs, Mom shakes her head. "You were never good enough for my daughter!"

"*Return!*" Helena howls, darting her hand into the black steam thickening above her, trying to capture her power back.

"It's not working!" Sascha yells. "It's not coming toward the ball."

"*Steal!*" Margo's mom calls out, running toward us. She puts her hand on Margo's. "Try *steal!*"

Mom, Mrs. Robbins, and Mrs. Ramirez dart over to us, and add their hands to the pile.

"*Steal!*" we yell together.

The moment the word leaves our lips, the black smoke spirals like a crazy tornado into the ball, and the portal collapses on itself.

Helena pushes herself up slowly. She stands, panting, with her hands clenched into tight little balls. The intense hate in her eyes tells me we'd be dead if the spell hadn't worked. "What've you done to me?" Her eyes stop on the orb I'm holding and yells, "*Retrieve!*"

I tense my grip around the ball, and then breathe out when it remains in my hand. I tap it with a finger, as a satisfied smile spreads across my face. "You can't hurt us anymore. You can't hurt anyone."

Helena's face contorts with rage. "*Retrieve!*" she screams again. When nothing happens she runs toward me. "Give me that ball!"

Mrs. Robbins blocks her way. "Take one more step and I'll call one of our vampire friends to finish you off. I'd bet they'd do it for free!"

Helena's mouth drops open in surprise.

"Hey!" Connor yells. "Everyone just calm down!" He starts for Mrs. Robbins, but the binder pulls him back in place.

Mrs. Robbins turns to Dani and opens her arms wide. Dani rushes in and Mrs. Robbins embraces her. "Can you ever forgive me?"

"Oh, shit! Oh, shit!" Zahara said. "*Another portal!*"

In the middle of the room, a small purple light hangs in the air, slowly growing.

"Ha!" Helena yells. "Ha! They're coming! You didn't think you could do this to me and not expect to pay!"

We all back away as she sidles up to the expanding portal, her face shining with unbridled glee.

I put the ball in my pocket and reach for my sword. "We're gonna need to work together!" I yell. "We need to get that thing before it can take any of us." My eyes connect with Mom's across the room. "I hope all of you moms remember how it's done!"

Mom smiles and nods, but I see tears in her eyes.

We form a circle around the portal with our mothers. Bile rises in my throat as the foul odor of brimstone turns my stomach and sears my nose. The room heats up as a large form begins to solidify in the middle of it, and I raise my sword.

Margo lets out a moan when a broad head with long, curved red horns comes into view.

My eyes nearly pop when a very large, and *very naked*, purple demon steps onto the meetinghouse floor—the tips of his horns skimming the ceiling. The choking, smoky odor envelops the room, and I grip my sword tighter so my shaking hands won't drop it.

"He's not wearing pants," Dani titters. "Wow!"

"Dani!" I hiss.

The demon scans the room and roars, spewing fire and smoke from his mouth.

"Go!" Margo yells, and she rushes at him swinging her ax.

I raise my sword, but before I move forward, the demon glares at Margo and she crumples to the floor, her ax turning to dust in her hands.

Margo's mother runs to her as Helena laughs. "This isn't some lesser demon roaming the earth! There is no weapon you can use!" Helena stares up into the demon's long, pointed face, her hands clutched tightly together at her chest. "Before you punish them," she says, "I need an item from that girl." She points to me and I gasp. "She has a glass ball with my powers. She stole my powers!"

The demon ignores Helena and locks his black, pupilless eyes with mine. "Greetings, hunter!" His rumbling voice makes the windows vibrate. "We have been most pleased with your work." He looks around at all of us, and smiles, revealing row upon row of sharklike teeth.

We exchange puzzled looks, and I see Sascha lower her sword a bit.

"Unfortunately . . . ," he says.

"Here it comes," Dani whispers.

I tense myself for a fight.

"The covenant has been irrevocably broken, and we have chosen not to negotiate a new one."

"Broken?" I ask with a cracking voice.

The demon locks eyes with mine again, and I shudder. "Six seconds ago an auction for the soul of a vampire was completed, and money wired to the coven account. As stated in the covenant, all souls gathered by you are the property of the Revealer realm," the demon continues. "As such, this blatant disregard for the covenant has terminated our agreement. All items held for us will be immediately collected."

"No!" Connor calls out. "I mean the auction finished,

but," he gulps nervously, "but they didn't kill the vampire, so the soul wouldn't have gotten sent to your realm. I didn't think it would count."

The demon narrows his eyes. "The coven accepted money for a soul. It counts."

Connor looks at Dani, and I silently beg him to stop talking so she can keep her soul—even if it is trapped in a ball. "I don't even have it anymore. She's got—"

Connor's eyes drift over to mine, and I shake my head. "Please," I whisper.

He takes a deep breath and turns back to the demon. "It's just gone."

Dani places her hand protectively over her pocket and bites her lip.

The demon shakes his head. "Whether you have lost possession of the soul or not, this coven brokered a deal for it!" he roars. Connor flinches, and then the demon tips his head at the rest of us and gives another sharky smile. "Enjoy the rest of your evening."

"Wait!" Dani calls out. "Does this mean we get to keep our souls?"

The demon scoffs. Smoke drifts from his mouth and nostrils, and I hold my breath waiting for him to answer. "It appears you've already lost yours, but as for the rest of you—no."

"What if we won't give them up?" I say, hoping he's not going to strike me down.

"When you die, be it today or a hundred years from now, your souls will be sent to the Revealer realm. There is nothing you can do," he states matter-of-factly.

I take out the balls containing Helena's power and the remaining poltergeist. "What if we gave you something in exchange for our souls?" I hold them up for him to see. "We have a ghost, and surely a witch's powers must be worth something."

"What? No!" Helena says. "Don't listen to—"

The demon turns on Helena, and she shrinks back as red flames shoot out of his mouth and nostrils toward her. "Silence!"

Helena falls to her knees, moaning and covering her head protectively with her arms. The smell of burnt hair mingles with the odor of brimstone.

He regards me again with his black, burning eyes. "Your souls are far more valuable than a witch's powers, and a ghost would be nothing, but—"

The ghost screams, and pushes its charred face up against the glass. The demon cocks its head and surveys the balls. He holds out a clawed hand as big as my head. "May I see them?"

Helena gasps, and looks up at me with pleading eyes. "No."

Her hair is singed on one side and a shudder racks through

me as I look at her raw, burnt scalp. I take a deep breath and remind myself that the demon could turn on me any second.

"Mom," Connor whispers.

I turn to Dani and she nods encouragingly. I walk toward the demon with trembling legs, trying not to choke on the overpowering odor swirling around him. I place the balls in one of his large palms, and my fingertips burn when they brush against his skin.

He holds one ball to the light and watches Helena's powers—still in the shape of a tornado—swirl around inside. Next, he takes the ghost ball in his other hand to examine. The poltergeist moans and bangs red, scarred fists on the glass, and the demon smiles.

"From time to time," he says, "we have matters on the earthly realm you could assist us with. If you would make yourselves available to us on a noncontractual basis, I will offer you the opportunity to earn back your souls. Should you agree, I would keep these," he says, rolling the balls in his fingers like marbles, "as a token of good faith between our realm and the coven."

I look at the other girls.

Dani shrugs. "I'll do whatever you want, Jules."

"I don't know," Zahara says.

"Me, neither," Sascha adds.

Margo, cradled in her mother's arms on the floor, shakes her head. "We can't do it again."

"Um," I begin nervously. "I think I can speak for all of us, and say if these *matters* involve collecting souls freelance, we're gonna have to pass."

The demon regards us all. "It's artifact collecting—something you've done for us in the past. Lesser demons frequently remove items from our realm to bargain with humans and other creatures, and we like to get them back."

"We could do that," Sascha says.

"You can't be seriously considering this?" Helena says. "After all your self-righteous prattle, you'd willingly work for them?"

"To get our souls back? Yeah, we would. But we're not signing anything," I say to the demon.

"Done then!" the demon says. He tosses the balls into the portal and bows his head.

"No!" Helena wails. She throws herself at his feet. "It was I who served you faithfully all these years. These girls didn't care about meeting your needs. It was all me! You must restore my power!"

He sighs and I can't take my eyes off the trails of smoke coming out each nostril. "I would have dealt with you in a more private setting. But as you insist on hounding me with the persistence of a nattering insect, I will reveal your punishment now." He looks at Helena and she doubles over, screaming.

"Jules, *someone*—help her!" Connor pleads.

Part of me wants to do something, but the fear of directing the demon's wrath at me keeps me frozen in place.

Helena looks up at the demon. "I've served you better than all of them," she sobs. "I don't deserve this."

"As coven leader, it was your responsibility to ensure the delivery of all souls to our realm." He holds his hand in the air, and a piece of parchment paper appears. He points to a sentence toward the bottom of the page with a long, pointed claw. "The forfeit of the covenant requires payment." He looks Helena in the eye, and two small flames flare out of his nose. "You."

"But it was Connor's idea!" she shrieks.

I jerk my head toward Connor, and see his mouth drop open.

"Mom! What are you doing?" he cries. He looks up at the demon with wide horrified eyes. "I didn't realize this would happen," he says quietly.

I point to the bindings on his legs. "*Release*!" The bindings fall, and I stand in front of him with my sword raised, shielding him from the demon. "He's not like her. Deep down, I know he isn't. Please, we'll work extra jobs for you, just don't take him!"

"If she says the boy was responsible, he must pay as well," the demon states. "And if you refuse to move I will simply go *through* you to get him."

"Jules, I really did love you," Connor whispers and kisses my cheek. "I wish we could do it all over again."

He steps out from behind me and approaches the demon.

"Stop!" I cry, but in a flash of purple and smoke, the demon, Helena, and Connor are gone.

Helena's scream echoes in the room as we stand there— mothers and daughters—a mix of shock and horror on our faces. I remember what Sascha said about her vision, and feel the deep sense of loss she described.

"Well, I'd say that nixes any chance of a reconciliation, but that would probably be inappropriate," Dani says.

Sascha jabs her with an elbow. "Shut up!"

I hang my head, and Mom takes me in my arms. I lean into her, smell her perfume, and sob as another feeling courses through me: regret. Because I can't help but wonder if Connor would still be here I hadn't tried to bargain for my soul.

EPILOGUE

I run my fingers along the newly hung graduation tassels swinging from the rearview mirror. "How many hours do you think it'll take?" I ask Michael.

"Factoring in all of the bathroom breaks we had to take when we tracked down that stuff for the demons over spring break"—he tilts his head slightly behind him toward Sascha— "I'm thinking ten hours to get to Bar Harbor."

Sascha leans forward right next to his ear, and takes a long drink off her water bottle. She swishes it around noisily in her mouth, and Michael swats a hand in her direction.

"Hey! I'm trying to drive," he says.

Sascha laughs as she settles back into her seat.

Michael reaches out and holds my hand. His touch sends shivers up my spine. I smile, thinking we'll celebrate our one-month anniversary during this trip. I wish Margo and Z had come, but I'm glad they're excited about starting college early.

"Look at the moon," I say as we round a corner. "Did you know it's almost full?" I call back to Finn jokingly.

"All werewolves keep track of the moon's cycle so they won't be taken by surprise," Dani says.

"*We know!*" Michael, Sascha, and I echo one another.

"Hey, stop picking on my girl, she can't help it if she's master of the obvious," Finn says.

"Hey!" Dani says.

"Ow!" Finn yells.

I look in the rearview mirror and think how surreal it is to only see Finn in the third-row seats even though Dani's there, too. Of course she's not used to not having a reflection yet, either, as she's always asking us if her hair looks OK. Michael takes a swig of his coffee and I think we have to do something to the van so the sun can't reach the back and we can start traveling during the day.

"How about we just stop worrying about the full moon," Dani says. "I told you there's a safe room at his grandmother's beach house, but it stinks I won't get to see my snuggims for one night of vacation."

"It's only *one* night," I say.

"Well, seeing as I can *only* see him at night, it stinks!"

I'm thinking a one-night reprieve from their constant

PDA will be nice. Loud, wet kissing sounds come from the backseat, and I cringe. I'd noticed a fairly fresh wound on Finn's neck before we left.

"*Please* tell me you're not snacking in the car, Dani?" I ask.

"*No, I'm not!*" she says.

"No sucking face in the car, either!"

"Yeah, get a room!" Sascha yells.

"You're just jealous," Dani says.

"Yeah, no." Sascha takes another swig off her water bottle. "Hey, did you hear Margo's mom got her real estate license? It's gonna be surreal seeing her squinty-eyed face on for sale signs around town."

I nod. "My mom told me."

"Hey, I finally checked out your mom's website," Sascha says. "I loved the description of the witch balls! Something about how they harken back to the days when it was believed witches and evil spirits roamed."

"Yeah, I got a kick out of that, too," I say. "They're actually selling really well, and she casts a spell on each one so if an evil spirit *did* show up at someone's house, it would get trapped in the ball."

"Speaking of which, did you get around to putting your ball in a safe deposit box yet, Dani?"

"My mom did—though I still don't see what was wrong with it sitting in my sock drawer."

"Maybe by the time we get home, someone will have found a spell to restore your soul," I say.

Dani scoffs. "I keep telling you all, I'm fine with the way things are, and I don't want the other vamps making fun of me. Besides, I'm a lot more fun now, right, snuggims?"

"You were fun before."

They giggle, and I shake my head. It'd be nice to have her soul back in place, if only to restore her inner censors.

"Well, hopefully we can locate the necklace quickly, get it to Mr. Big Naked Purple Guy, and then start some partying," Sascha says.

"Yeah," I agree. "I'm still burnt-out from finals."

"At least you got to take them," Dani says.

I turn around and look back at Dani. "Are you serious? You were forever stressing out and complaining about tests!"

"But I liked the grades afterward. And getting a GED is not the same as standing on the stage getting a diploma."

"Trust me, you didn't miss a thing," Michael says. "It was like ninety degrees in the gym, and Evan's valedictorian speech about ships getting ready to set sail was riddled with clichés. I was hoping one of you would throw a spell at him and end our misery!"

Finn laughs. "I wanted to tell him to keep it short, but after I told him Dani and I hooked up, I'm not exactly his favorite person."

"He's being such a baby about it," Dani says. "*He's* the one who dumped me—he didn't even give the *new me* a chance."

I look out the window and wonder for the millionth time about Connor. Would I have given him another chance? I shake my head. Probably not. Too much had happened, and being able to trust someone implicitly—like Michael—shows me what I was missing.

I watch the moon whip by just above the trees on the side of the road. It's been seven months since Connor was taken away, and I still have nightmares each and every night about what might be happening to him. I can't help but feel guilty, like I should have done more to stop it. Especially since it was Connor's mistake that freed the rest of us.

Sort of.

I glance at the rolled-up parchment the demon—whose purple hue prompted Dani to dub him "Brimstone Barney"—gave us. The necklace is with a human, which means breaking and entering instead of slicing and dicing. And with Dani's morphing ability it should be a fairly easy task.

Who knows how long we'll be working for the demon, but at least there's hope of a *soulful* death, and that's something worth living for.

Here's a peek at another
novel by Amanda Marrone:

UNINVITED

I close my eyes, hoping he won't come tonight. It's later than usual. I hope he's given up, or just gone, and I can finally sleep. Cool air blows through the window, and I marvel at my bravery. Or stupidity. It's opened just a crack, no more than an inch. But until tonight I've kept it closed, so I know he'll be wondering what it means.

I listen for some movement in the branches outside, but the leaves are dry and noisy now. I open my eyes—I have to look. It's better when I see him coming. I put every ounce of energy into listening, waiting for my eyes to adjust to the dark. I turn my head, grimacing at the sound of my long hair against the pillowcase. I look out my window, searching the branches, wondering if he'd still come if I chopped down the tree.

"Jordan, are you awake?"

My heart races as I hunt for Michael among the branches. His dark form is pressed against the trunk a few feet higher from his usual perch. How long has he been watching me? He drops down, settling in closer to the window, and I remind myself to look for an ax in the morning.

"Jordan, let me in."

"Go away, Michael. I will never let you in." My voice is steady and calm, without emotion. I've said these words a hundred times today, so they'd become automatic. So I wouldn't change my mind.

Michael sighs, and I think I see him nodding. He knows I'm not ready to let him in. I suspect he knows I think about it, though. I suspect he knows that a part of me wants to.

"You don't know how good you have it, Jo."

I don't like where this is leading. This won't be a "let's talk about the future" night. Michael's missing his old life and he'll keep me up for hours if I encourage him.

"Did you go to school today? Did anyone talk about me?"

I roll my eyes. "This is high school, Michael, you're old news. People have found better things to gossip about. I mean, dying in the summer . . . well, your timing was way off. If having people remember you is important, that is. There's just way too much happening, people move on pretty quickly. Now, if you had died during the school year, that would have made a bigger impact."

"God, Jo! This isn't easy for me, you know."

I nod and wonder if his eyes see better than mine. Can he see I'm putting on an act, that every inch of my skin tingles when he sits outside my window? "I'm sorry, Michael, but I'm tired. I need to sleep."

"But I miss you, Jo. It's not like you think. I can't sleep. I can't sleep at all. I'm awake with nothing to do. Nothing to do but think, and miss you."

"I'll leave some books outside for you tomorrow. Maybe you can accomplish something you never did when you were alive—you can actually read a book. Or, hey, how about this? You can walk into the sunlight and end this all. Have you thought of that? What would happen if you walked into the sun?"

Michael's quiet, and I think he may keep it short tonight—until he taps his foot on my window.

"How's Steve and Eric?" he asks. "They still playing ball?"

"Oh God." I turn my back to the window. "Ask me something I care about. Your stupid friends are exactly the same as they were when you were alive. They live and breathe football or basketball or whatever stupid ball season it is. They still hang out with their gorgeous girlfriends and they still smash mailboxes after a few too many beers. I'm surprised you haven't joined them. That was one of your favorite pastimes, wasn't it?"

He doesn't answer, and I remember Michael making

out with some girl—one hand up her short skirt, pressing her against the lockers—acting like he wasn't making an ass of himself. I wonder how many guys walking past dreamed of trading places with Michael? I know how often I dreamed of trading places with that girl.

"So, what, they don't talk about me? Like, not at all?"

He's definitely not letting it go tonight. I think he actually thought they'd worship him forever.

I turn back to the window, but I remember to move slowly this time. I've seen my cat throw itself against the window trying to catch the birds outside in the tree. I sometimes wonder if Michael will lose patience with me and begin to think of me like that, like a bird. Like his prey. So I move bit by bit because I don't know what I would do if Michael were to throw himself against the glass.

"I lied before," I finally say. "Everyone talks about you. They actually talk about you a lot." I pause and let Michael think what he will. "But they're not reminiscing. They think you killed yourself." I've wanted to tell Michael this for a long time, but he was such a mess over the summer, it didn't seem right. But tonight I'm feeling mean, and I won't baby him. Besides, he doesn't seem to care about what his visits do to me.

"What? Who thinks that?"

"Everyone. Everyone at school. And I've been wondering, too." I bite my lip, deciding if I should go on.

"I've told you what happened," he says sharply. "You know what I was dealing with. There's no way I could have stopped it."

I've been wondering if that's true, but I can't tell him that—not yet. "Well, they think you killed yourself and they talk about why you did it. And not just your friends. Everyone."

I let my words sink in. I let him mull over the thought of the entire school ignoring his football record in favor of gossip.

"You wouldn't believe the theories that went around. Some were really laughable. 'Michael was bipolar.' 'Michael only had one month to live.' But don't feel too bad, it was purely defensive. People needed to find the flaws they'd missed when you were alive, because if the great Michael Green couldn't handle things, how is everybody else supposed to?"

"Well, at least you know the truth," he says.

I've wounded him and catch myself before a satisfied smile emerges on my face. I'm long past trying to understand what Michael does to me. Making me wish he were here in my room—in my bed—again, then the next minute making me relish the hurt in his voice. But I won't beat myself up for bruising his ego. He's made me his prisoner every night, and I'm glad when I can get a dig in.

"Damn it!" he growls, startling me. "I'm sick of talking. Let me in!"

He suddenly shifts his weight and slaps his palms against the glass. I flinch like it's me he's hit. I try to shrink away from him and sink into the mattress. God, why did I say those things?

My mouth dries to paper as I suck in the cold air pouring in over the sill. I make myself as small as possible and freeze into place. So far the window has barred his way. But that damn inch. I imagine him with new cat eyes that can see in the dark, noticing the currents of air playing around the opening. Does he know what I did—can he see? Is that small opening invitation enough for him to enter?

"Jordan," he croons. "I'm sorry. I'm so sorry. I didn't mean to scare you. I just miss you so much. I just want to be with you."

He jumps down to the ground, and I melt into the bed.

I'm shaking, but I won't pull up the blanket. I need to feel the cold; I need to feel something besides the ache I get when he leaves me. I hate myself for wanting him, for feeling flattered it's me he haunts every night.

Three months now I've talked to him through the window. Three months I've conjured his face from the time when he was mine. I see his chestnut eyes, his brown curls, his white, white teeth, and full mouth. I put that face on over the shadows and imagine we could start over.

But the leaves are falling and soon Michael will sit on bare branches. Moonlight will finally find its way to his face, and I'll see what I know is true: that Michael is a monster.

I'm just afraid that one of these nights I might let him in.

AMANDA MARRONE grew up on Long Island where she spent her time reading, drawing, watching insects, and suffering from an overactive imagination. She earned a BA in education at SUNY Cortland and taught fifth and sixth grades in New Hampshire. She now lives in Connecticut with her husband, Joe, and their two kids.

PULSE it

Did you **love** this book?

Want to get the
hottest books **free**?

Log on to
www.SimonSaysTEEN.com
to find out how you can get
free books from **Simon Pulse**
and become part of our **IT Board**,
where you can tell **US**, what **you** think!

SIMON
PULSE